Praise for
Rain Check

Beautifully rendered, the stories in *Rain Check* could well be the footprints and photographs of our own lives if we'd have taken risks as daring as Noe's characters. Each misstep, triumph and regret rings true. Reading these stories is like being a lucky voyeur who happens upon an artist with brush in hand, nearing the finishing touch of their masterpiece. Nothing is more potent than prose that lifts off the page and lands, like a well-placed bullet or caress, on the heart, and that's precisely what Noe has done here.

~ Len Kuntz, author of *Dark Sunshine* and *I'm Not Supposed to be Here and Neither Are You*

Levi Andrew Noe has a supernatural handle on what the forces of nature mean—every blade of bent grass, big fat raindrop and purple storm cloud ripping across the surface of this odd earth. By extension of understanding animal instinct he knows humanity from the tip of its nose to the curled hook of its trigger finger. Mostly, though, Noe does that thing too few writers of fine literature do—he draws us into adventures that lie outside of the quiet interior human life. We're led up a mountain for a closer look at a golden moon.

~ Bud Smith, author of *Calm Face*, *Tollbooth* and *Everything Neon*

Noe's Flash Fiction collection is divided into three sections, where despair and hope are prevalent themes. These stories called me to greedily read one after another. They are connected by the humanity of the characters and situations. Noe's ability to show these attributes can't be praised high enough while using empathy and humor.

~ Paul Beckman, author of *Peek*

The tiny, potent stories that make up this debut by Levi Andrew Noe both surprise and delight. There's wisdom in these pages, but also humor, tenderness, and magic. *Rain Check* is a terrific read from a young author to watch.

~ Kathy Fish, author of *Wild Life*, *Rift* and *Together We Can Bury It*

Levi Andrew Noe is a modern-day Beat. The stories in this collection are meditative and mystical, his characters full of spirit. From the streets of suburban Colorado to the rivers of the Himalayas, Noe makes you feel the wanderlust, the backpack straps tugging at your shoulders, the hunger to connect with all that's come before and all that's yet to come.

~ Steve Karas, author of *Kinda Sorta American Dream*

RAIN CHECK

STORIES BY

LEVI ANDREW NOE

TRUTH SERUM PRESS

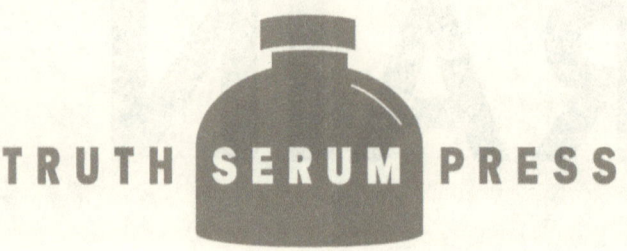

ISBN: 978-1-925536-09-6

Truth Serum Press
4 Warburton Street
Magill SA 5072
Australia

Email: truthserumpress@live.com.au
Website: http://truthserumpress.net
Truth Serum Press catalogue: http://truthserumpress.net/catalogue/

Cover photograph is in the public domain and can be found here:
https://pixabay.com/en/mountain-lake-person-looking-view-931726/

Author photograph by Kadi Spurlock / Up in the Sycamore Photography

Also available as an eBook
ISBN: 978-1-925536-10-2

This book is dedicated to

Hannah

and all our years
and rain checks to come.

Contents

On Time and Place

On Relations

On Mind, Body, Heart and Soul

ON TIME
AND PLACE

The Price You Pay

When you leave home, you pay with your heart. For every place you go there is a price for all you see, taste, touch, love. Every time your heart opens and accepts, there is a heart toll.

In this way nothing is without cost, and nothing is lost, or taken for granted.

When the woman sitting beside you on the plane told you this, it stuck with you. Whether or not you believed it, since then you've always carried your heart a little heavier with the change to pay for this vast world of heartache and wonder.

A Sunrise to See
Before You Die

I remember racing the dawn on borrowed bicycles through the volley of horns aimed like arrows at us through the traffic that was at every moment as destructive and unpredictable as a flooded river.

And then we stopped, turned the locks and hurried to the highest view to watch the sun rise over Angkor Wat.

I've read bucket lists, things to do before you die, and this was on the list. I've always felt like such imperatives were foolish, an oxymoron, to live life ringed around death.

I saw the crimson bleed into the edge of the moat and the low clouds ignited like God's no vacancy signs in magenta and neon pink on the horizon. I made a mark on my own list. And as I watched a billion year old star rise over a millennia old temple complex I burned my list, yet again.

Three Scenes

I

Wet feet, wet clothes, wet hair. Drenched. It's raining hard, but the redwoods catch most of it. The streams swell and babble boisterously, drunk on the downpour. I test my step on the mossy rocks, see a salamander doing the same. It's gray, and green, and red in all directions. I'm soggy-lost, but trust that I'll find the path again.

II

Sharp morning breath; awake, alone in a quiet canyon of the Sangre de Cristos just north of Crestone.

The Arkansas sang me to sleep and now drowsily rouses me to let the dawn in.

Evergreens and aspen shake off the cold of the night with some help from the wind.

The forest a commotion of tree chatter, but no goodbyes. The branches waving aren't for me as I pack up camp, uproot, to hitch back home.

III

One night walking the bare desert looking for warmth we found so easily with the sun's blaze. Best to just find soft sand and burrow into sleeping bags.

Tomorrow we will find the hot springs with some help from the day, clearer eyes and signposts.

Tonight, just sleep and dream of belonging under the stars.

New York, New York

A pigeon roost, a satellite dish, a car bumping reggae on the street below, gardens of graffiti, thousands of century old brick buildings in every direction, millions of people from every continent; and a rusted lawn chair on an apartment roof off St. John's in Brooklyn. Here, I can see it all—well—most of it.

No, I'm barely scratching the surface.

Five Points

The man in the bedazzled western wear smokes across the street from the bearded man in a mini-skirt who walks past the market of artisans and healers. There, in the square of asphalt where, nightly, drunks come to drown, pimps come to hustle, and pushers come to poison the veins of a gentrified neighborhood where gangs have been bangin' for decades and business is booming for entrepreneurs.

I sit behind my table at the market selling natural health and body care products, and self-published children's books wondering how this all possibly fits. And if there's any way to reconcile our differences.

16th and California

On the corner of the concrete city, a brunch-full sun warms the street to an unseasonal 70 in early March. Pale people, dark people, polished and smudged, wearing rags, wearing black suits, with gravestone faces, smiles ear to ear; with eyes peering, red, squinted, wide, fearful.

The sun—neutral—divides the street nearly exactly in half; into yellow puddles of warmth and shadow. People choose to walk on one side or pass through the boundary. They notice, or don't, going where they go.

Classical symphonies play at the light rail stop to deter loiterers. The train bell blares through the soupy din of sirens, humans, wind, engines. Everything comes together to make music that no one but the beggar on the corner seems to hear, shuffling his feet in a dance.

Long Road

It's a long road from here to there.

A government bus painted in prayers and rust, Himalayan road curling like a serpent. Too many twists and turns to sleep, too terrified to stay awake. You gave me the better seat while you stared down at the canyon. I never thought that night would end, but 16 hours later we're walking on the clouds.

I took a train out of Bangkok. On my own, I took the town in. There were monkeys and ancient temples and kids kicking bottles in the street. I still remember the heat so well, always made me feel like I didn't belong. I think it's funny and sometimes sad what we forget and remember.

I can still see you on the Mekong. Hammock, beer and a guitar. We were singing with all our hearts *Proud Mary* by CCR.

It's a long road, from there to here.

A Room with a View

A room with a view meant a 15-minute hike up meandering stairs through the town of Vishisht carrying 50 pounds on our backs. You had me at 200 rupees a night and the knotted back was normal by now. I followed and we found a mattress without too much mold. I felt better here, stronger, invigorated, even after the 16 hour sleepless bus ride winding through crumbling Himalayan roads. When I looked down at the valley etched out by the river and the mountain peaks, jagged as sharks teeth, I knew what I'd been missing.

The Ganga

I remember the day I jumped into the river. High in the Himalayas, I felt like water and I had never met before. I swam against it, pushed back the current that would always win in the end. And I didn't know why I had waited so long to jump in. Was it the pollution or the river's source that I was more scared of?

It had been the hottest, hardest summer. I had been further, lived fuller than I'd ever lived. And the water, the water is what I remember most. Coming from Colorado, thousands of miles from either ocean, water carries a different weight. I swam in the Pacific, the East China Sea, the Gulf of Thailand, flowed with the Mekong, bathed in waterfalls in Thailand and Laos, soaked in dozens of onsens in Japan and saw colors of water that I thought only existed in fantasy. But why had I been by the Ganga for over a month and only then jumped in?

Maybe I was simply waiting for the right time to be baptized and born again. Or was it the holy river telling me I was always clean and free from sin? Or maybe, it was all these maybes that needed to learn for themselves how to sink or swim.

Same, Same, but Different

A Thai pepper plucked fresh from the bush. "You taste," said my guide. I bit in with something to prove and then drank, in one gasping gulp, all the water I had for the hike through the jungle and elephant ride to the hill tribe.

Rice fields in the sticky summer, endless in every direction. Mt. Tsukuba in the background holding up the sky.

Two days traveling by slow-boat. Sitting right next to the motor doesn't drown out the green beauty and the river's song pulling me into this artery of the earth, the Mekong.

People, animals, rivers, mountains, trains, temples everything from the cow dung to the holy men all living and breathing with a vividness that hurts at first until I accept it for what it is, and then the Himalayas feel like my oldest home.

Sakura trees on every street, every field, every path, and climbing to the clouds on every mountain. The ethereal pink-white blossoms that light up the earth and sky are a color that can only be seen once a year for one week, maybe two, if you're lucky; or in rare, promising dreams.

Two years later when I come back home. It is autumn and the aspen in the Rockies are a gold and ochre ocean. It's a cloudless day and the moon rests on the hips of the mountains. I think of that grove of trees sharing a single source, and I feel my own roots circle the earth.

Southeast Asia Blues

He took the 50-pound bag off his back. For the hundredth time Jack thought about the last time, somewhere in the un-dreamable future, when he would take that bag off for good. How his shoulders would weep with joy. He hated the hurt, how the hurt made him complain, how the complaints made him regret, and how the regret drove him to homesick laments. Traveling, at least his kind of wandering way, was a weary business. Jack had to give the aches and pains their place in this adventure. It was only fair.

The door opened and his incidental bunkmate, traveling companion and compatriot in rowdy unruliness stepped into the dank room. Two twin beds, semi-clean sheets just waiting to be dampened by their sweat-soaked bodies, a bathroom on the other side of a paper thin wall next to one bed, a dresser filled with dead cockroaches, spiders' webs in most, if not all, of the corners, a ceiling fan missing two blades and a rusted window with no screen.

"Nice place." Axel headed straight for the shower. "Lordy, Lordy, am I glad to be off that bus. I think the guy next to me crapped his pants. If I wasn't as tired as I was I think I might have been tempted to vomit right into his crap-stained lap. Luckily I was passed out the majority of that ride."

"Yea. Five bucks a night isn't bad. And we're right by the river. What river is that? What country are we even in?"

"It's the river Kwai, that's the bridge to Terabithia, and we're in Narnia." Axel stripped down to his boxer shorts exposing pink, sun-scorched flesh striped like a zebra.

"Right. So shall we see what Narnia has to offer once we're settled in here?"

"Always with the plans." Axel stretched like a tiger just waking up to a jungle hangover. "Let's just head to 7-11 in a bit so I can pick up some of that disgusting rice wine and then grab a bite. We'll see what we see."

"Right."

Axel retreated to the shower and Jack to his bed. Jack reached into his pack for a few essentials. He loathed that bag at this moment. Though he was not so loathsome that he did not remember the landlocked days of wanderlust when dreams of travel were his only escape. He lay down on the bed, which he had been sure to check for mold, blood, and bed bugs before laying down. He held in his hand a 5-year-old iPod, and a postcard.

He had only 10 minutes or so to ache and to wallow before Axel came out to shake him from his meta-emo-contemplation. It was good to have a man like Axel as his travelling partner. Jack could disappear for days into some inner landscape and fail to extract the sense of awe and beauty from his exotic surroundings if not properly goaded. Axel was just the man to keep him from withdrawing into more comfortable, shadowy surroundings.

Only 8 minutes or so left. Jack was having a hard time deciding on the proper music to accompany his few remaining moments of despondency. He settled on Deathcab for Cutie. He could now being to examine the postcard for the hundredth time. There was a photograph from the 1920s or '30s. Several boys in scarves, caps, coats and mittens posing with their wooden steel-runner sleds. It felt terribly out of place with his present tropical, muggy surroundings, which was the point, it seemed. He nearly fell in to the photograph, feeling the frozen nose, dripping snot and the pulsing, beating sparrow's heart of young children in their most boundless states of excitement.

He had only 6 minutes left. He turned the postcard and read the words he had memorized forwards and backwards.

My Wanderer,

Your last letter makes it sound like you are having adventures that most people only dream about. But I hear your sadness, or maybe just homesickness, behind the words. You can't conceal anything from me. I don't know why you still try. Your living the story of a lifetime right now. Your living your dreams. Your going to look back on this time when your older and be so happy to have these memories. Don't forget that ok? Just keep reminding yourself. Think about how much your going to have to write about. Your the most beautiful person I know, but I know you don't see it that way. I don't care, I love the way you are.

Love,
Cadence

P.S. I didn't want to say how much I missed you because I want you to keep enjoying yourself. But it's not the same without you here.

He put the letter down and pretended to be annoyed by her "yours" just to keep emotional control. He only had 2 minutes. He knew she was right. About everything. She always was. And soon he knew that he would be laughing and drinking in another stunning, vivid town. He'd be soaking in the air and street food and colorful people of a new place. But for now he wanted to put his hands on his chest and see if he could heal the tender parts of his heart in the same way a cheap Thai massage took care of his aching muscles. If only it were that simple.

The shower door opened, steam swirled out congealing with the muggy air. Jack pretended to just be waking from a power nap.

"Let's do this," Jack hoped he sounded sincere.

"That's what I'm talking about. Let's hijack a tuk-tuk and cross the border to Burma!" Axel hollered.

"Yea, or let's just start with dinner."

"K, either way. Hey, do you have that magic powder? I'm chafing somethin' fierce, if you know what I mean."

Jack handed Axel the Snake Brand Prickly Heat cooling powder and put away the postcard without it being seen. It would be safe until the next time he needed reminding.

Thumb Out

Thumb out like a wet match, a cardboard sign that says 'Home'. All I own in my backpack. Counting the cars as they pass. Can't they see? I'm in need of something: the open road, windows down, endless horizon, distance, movement, a place to rest my feet, rest my eyes. If not I can always pitch a tent, unroll my mat. Where I sleep, there's my bed.

Not asking for much, only everything free. And for today I'll be satisfied with just a ride along the way to where I'm going.

First Hitch

It was easier than I thought, this hitchhiking business. I walked only ten or fifteen minutes, holding a cardboard sign that said 'Denver', when I got my first ride. I was leaving Taos, New Mexico headed back home because, well, I missed my mom. I had been having bad dreams, seeing her suffer or die for the past couple weeks. I didn't really believe my nightmares, but I had been gone for over four months, and you know how mothers worry.

The first ride didn't get me very far, just far enough that I couldn't walk back to Taos, so I stuck out my thumb. Five minutes and my next ride came.

All right, I thought, *I'll be home before dark.*

"Be safe!" the older gentleman shouted at me, pulling away. I got two more rides without waiting longer than ten minutes. I had traveled perhaps fifty miles, left alone at a gas station off a desolate two lane highway, still south of the Colorado border. I was too excited to sit still at the gas station so I continued walking. It was dry and hot, the end of spring in the high mountain desert. I walked two or three miles when I saw the first house I'd seen since the gas station. Its only inhabitant that I saw, a dog, barked at me. I was bored, I barked back. This dog did not like that. He ran toward me from his fenceless yard. I kept walking, he approached closer and closer, barking more and more viciously, baring teeth, drooling. I raised myself up, turned toward him and he would stand down briefly, then he would get closer, louder, more aggressive. *I've never had to fight a dog before*, I analyzed the situation, *I don't know who would win, but if this son of a bitch* (no pun intended) *means business, I won't hold back.*

Just when I thought I was going to have to make my move, a large pickup truck comes roaring down the highway and distracts the dog. He turns from me, hypnotized by the truck and wanders onto the road. 75 miles an hour comes at you faster than you'd expect. I can still hear that sound, metal on flesh and bone. The dog was carried twenty feet. I knew what I would see: eyes open, blood leaking from his mouth, dead instantly. I told the family, who seemed less affected than I was. I felt cursed, I left the house crying and continued walking bleakly down the highway. I saw it as an ominous sign, I walked almost fifteen miles without a ride.

Mount Madonna

The redwoods wake at night, rustling tree tendrils—restrained, watching, every branch has eyes. Paths shift like snakes in the darkness; drifting light from the moon swells and retreats as clouds pass. Shadows walk like wind on the edge of my vision.

Every needle's twitch makes me jump; over-alert ears mistake stillness. The deep dream odor of sap and damp earth, of fallen tree fingers turning over the soil.

I walked alone, calling for company, but feared the answer.

Eyes, Ears, Feet and Faith

I wandered on a walk, wondering where I'd find the path among the maze of redwoods. But then there it was, along with a class of kindergartners.

"Won't you join us?" the teacher asked.

"Sure," so I fell in line.

First there was the pond.

"It's so much fuller!" Mouths wide at the work of the rain.

As we walked, two boys spoke of lizards.

"Its belly was red."

"No, it was a yellow bellied newt."

At the sound of the stream the teacher hushed the crowd.

"Be quiet," a soft commandment. "Do you hear it? Isn't it wonderful? The more silence we have, the louder *it* gets."

The class clambered on, forging streams, conquering puddles. All along the way the teacher chided the students who got too far, or hovered too near the path's edges. At a bend the teacher stilled the children, told us to shut our eyes.

"All right, now, listen. Are everyone's eyes closed? Are everyone's ears open? Do you hear it?"

The river sang somewhere down below.

"Now, do you see it, even with your eyes closed?"

I peeked, the whole class nodded.

"There are some things that are there, even though we can't see them. Isn't it strange? OK, you can open your eyes."

The children looked out now, eyes brighter than ever, all the more full of wonder.

"Look, you still can't even see the river from here but somehow, some way, you're sure that it's there. This is good to remember later when you're lost, finding your way."

She looked at me.

Without a word she turned, the class followed faithfully. I lingered a bit longer, still listening for the river.

Remembering Rain

Remembering rain on a two lane highway crawling up the coast of Ketchikan, Alaska, a temperate rainforest island. And the wind that always seemed to be pushing against me no matter which way I was riding, on a bike that always seemed to have a flat, or a shifting issue or a gear grinding.

And by the time I got to my job at the coffee shop, 7 miles out of town at 6 a.m., I was drenched, exhausted and empty. Always in between waking and dreaming because I hadn't been sleeping well with the summer sun only setting for a few hours of twilight and then rising before the night could come, though you would never know it with the clouds and the rain and the gray.

And I remember asking myself why had I come? What was I doing? What was I proving and to whom? I never got a reply when I was expecting it, but weeks passed, my mind and body adjusted and then the land answered. After the rain, the forest burst out with flowers and berries and salmon and black bears, and the view over inlets and narrow straights of rugged, untouched red cedar and sitka spruce covered mountains jutting from the ocean and nights where we stayed up until two when the sun set; and devil's club, and canning the season and bald eagles and ravens and finding friends sharing the same dreams of wanderlust.

So, now, whenever it rains I ask for more, and I remind myself what the gray means and what the clouds carry. I remember bike rides at 5 a.m. with views I'll never see anywhere else ever again and dreams blooming inside me sewing seeds that will always be with me, just waiting for the rain.

Denver RTD

I'm working, technically, job coaching. On the 52 bus taking a student to a new job at the Aztlan Rec Center. I know something is off about this day, it's warm and muggy, nice cloud cover. Opposite day in Denver. People are too nice. Instead of the usual clamor, eerie silence, or alcohol-sweat stank, people are talking. A young man is asking where the indoor mall is on 16th St. Someone answers, and the conversation continues. The young man keeps up the questions, places to go, cafés, galleries, quality times to be had, and the whole scene is so innocent and honest that I feel like I'm in another place, or at least another dimension.

I ride back by myself, reading a book, *The Science of Yoga*, when the man next to me asks if I do yoga. The man has a torn sleeveless shirt, covered in tattoos and hard knocks.

"Yes," I say.

"What kind?" he asks.

"All kinds." I still don't know how to answer this question.

"I did yoga in prison," he informs me.

"Neat," I say. "What was that like?"

"Good," he begins, "I did it for two months. I practice magic so it was, like, good for that, the asanas and the breathing. But it just ain't the same without the women."

"Right," I say. I laugh, awkward and nervous.

I'm very glad to be having this conversation, but I'm a little frightened.

"Welp, see ya later."

I get off at 17th and Tremont, walk back to work past the courthouse.

Later, I'm still working, taking the light rail to Colfax at Auraria with another student. A girl in the seat across from me asks, "How's your day going?"

"Great," I say.

My student smiles. She seems nice, but this student and I have been working on how to safely interact with strangers. I am teaching him the RTD system and city safety. He is 28 with Down Syndrome and has been getting lost in Five Points at night. The girl then pulls an albino rat out of her pocket. The smile on his face is priceless, we're both laughing hard. It's the perfect distraction because he's still learning his stops and so I ask him how many stops we are away. One, he holds up a finger, correctly. The girl then proceeds to kiss her rat. The rat affectionately nibbles on her lip.

"Here's our stop," he says.

Maigo

What better sickness
than to lose the voice from love
and karaoke?

There is no better time to be had than to gather a group of friends in a small, windowless room, stand on couches, sing out of key with blind fury and keep the servers running back and forth ordering from the all-you-can-drink menu. Karaoke in Japan, the stuff foreigner's dreams are made of.

It was a successful night. About six hours of non-stop sing-screaming and non-stop drinking. Our voices hoarse and bloody, our eyes crossed, unfocused, we stumbled into the muggy Japanese night thoroughly inebriated at 3 a.m.

"We're going to McDonalds!" one vociferous Englishman cried out.

The others slurred out their approval, but I, as always, wanted to take the path less travelled. Before anyone noticed or did a head count, I had slipped off, certain that I could find my way home through the back roads. I found a pedestrian trail that I thought I recognized. It was beside a small river and there were rice fields and small groupings of traditional Japanese houses on either side. It looked familiar to me, but that was because everything in my prefecture, Ibaraki, looked like that. I was only two months in to my Japanese life, so much to learn.

Before I came to Japan I had two pictures in my mind of what this land could look like. The first was the soaring, swarming, labyrinthine megalopolis of Tokyo. The second was the quaint, rustic countryside with Mt. Fuji ever-present in the background. I was partially correct, but I could have never imagined what the majority of Japan would look like. Envision an endless stretch of strip malls on either side of every major road. These roads with no names, only numbers, were the main veins and arteries of the inaka, or countryside, of Japan. Now, off these more major thoroughfares were an endless number of arterioles, capillaries, venules and other tributaries that could lead to anywhere just as easily as they could to nowhere. These smaller roads led to the true countryside of Japan, the marshy rice paddies, the small towns that seemed preserved from the 1800's and the mountain roads that meandered up the lost mountains of time. However, these minor byways rarely had names or numbers, which, when giving directions, leads to a series of absurd routes based on landmarks, convenience stores and other courses that only a seasoned captain versed in nautical navigation could translate.

This is all to say that I was not going to find my way home that night. Luckily for me I had asked my employers to write down my address in Japanese. Within my first week of attempting to make sense of the road system in Japan I anticipated this eventuality. I turned around after a quarter mile or so, at least wise enough to know when I was ass-backward-lost. I returned to the 50, the main street in my town, Shimodate. I stumbled up to the first living thing I saw. Luckily it was a human with a car. A young man and a pretty Japanese woman tried hard to mask the horror and revulsion of seeing my foreign, stuporous face. In my best Japanese at the time I said something like:

"Sssumimassen gaaa, umm, shit. Sssummimassenn. Maigo desu. Yea, that's the word. Maigo. Umm, hold on..."

I had managed to communicate that I wished to be excused and that I was a lost child. I pulled the address out of my wallet and handed it to the man. In hindsight I had most likely been a major cock-block to their evening. They spoke in a language as foreign to me as Martian, and the man gestured for me to enter his car. They said goodbye to each other, and I said "Arigatoooo!" too many times to count.

The man took me promptly to my apartment. I tried to pay him money, but he politely refused and gestured to the door. Again I said "Arigatooo," "Arigato gozaimashita," far too many times.

I stumbled to my doorstep. Everyone else had made it back to their respective sleeping places already and did not seem too worried about my whereabouts. I fell asleep on my futon, the smell of the tatami mat lulling me to a drunken doze. The next morning I would tell my companions of my first and only time hitchhiking in Japan. But while a fleeting flicker of consciousness remained in me I would thank the nameless man who saved this pale, lost child.

Self-Made Secret Agent

Sometimes in subway stations, or college campuses, or hip cafés, or on top of mountains I sit or stand with contorted face, blank piece of paper in hand and pretend like I am waiting for someone, or following clandestine instructions on a note.

In places I've never been or places I've been a thousand times, I flip some switch or dim some inner sun and let myself feel like I don't belong. And once my belonging has unhinged I can feel at home as a man on the run. And then I pretend like I'm waiting for a sign from the sky, or I've got some mission, so secret that even I don't know it yet.

And I'm just there acting nonchalant, carrying on like any other normal citizen, but really I'm posting out waiting for that call to come through from the payphone across the street or the man in sunglasses to come pass me a flash drive and a note that says:

"For your eyes only."

A Chorus of Winter

A chorus of winter snows down. It's a cold song, it's slow and it stings when you open your ears to it, but it's too melancholy and lovely to leave alone, or turn down the volume.

The gray, the white, the brown of bare trees. The gasp of sharp breath, the crack of dry skin; the longing for a fire to share with someone, the emptying, the solitude.

All this, alive in the air and the seasons' unseen conductor never sleeps, never misses a beat; the deathless choir never stops singing this flawless dream—ever-same, ever-changing.

Retreat

Lately I'm all distant dreams, all white cold and cave-hunched, all bare branched, all roots, and stew, all blue fire; all inside myself. I'm waiting at a train station in the Siberian isolation of my mind.

I issue tickets to all my fractured selves. They come to me empty eyed, ribs, knees and elbows sharp with hunger and survival. They come for sleep, for a warm meal, for the forgetting of their stories. And I send them off to silent retreats in the Himalayas or to paint in the desert, perhaps to visit an old friend in the Pacific Northwest. They come back in time and if they have healed what needed healing, then they rest inside me, and we attempt to love unconditionally as we wait for the weary and the self-loathing, and the broken to seek the cure in the pain.

This is how I wait for wholeness and the passing of time and solitude. This is my reply when you ask where I've been lately.

On the Equinox

Salamanders danced with fireflies. The sun and moon aligned for a date at twilight, for which the sky prepared an eleven-course meal while the ocean bartended.

Summer and autumn met at a campfire on the equator and shared a bottle of mead over some stories.

But there was no one, no one in all of creation who was more acutely aware of the earth's orbit on this day than the man by the river who slept on wet cardboard, burlap blanket with feet uncovered. He woke at dawn and took a leak in some bushes to come back to his makeshift bridge bedroom and exclaim:

"The Holy Grail! It's missing!"

But after a few minutes of trying to find it and failing he shuffled to the river, put his feet in the water, saw the sunrise reflecting over the flowing mirror and sighed with relief.

"Ah, never mind. There it is again."

ON
RELATIONS

Rain Check

I remember you taking your rain check from me beside the stream, the chanterelles, the devil's club, making a bed from our clothes. You let out your love like clouds full of rain and your voice rose to the tops of the Sitka spruce. You looked like you belonged there in the moss and dark, damp earth. A wild geranium.

And I felt like the outsider, an invasive weed with no place in a temperate rainforest. This inland-man from the high plains. You knew this, and still, you took me into you. Watching me turn like a leaf in the fall.

Bear Creek

I wanted to take a walk down by the water. There was that certain light that only autumn can create and the yellow on the cottonwood trees looked so warm to me.

Watching water bugs do what only holy men are supposed to be able to, I searched for patterns in the current. Anything that could add up, bring me closer to the comfort of answers, or glimpses of the great design. I tested the creek's flow with rocks to see if they would skip or sink, they mostly sank. Still not satisfied, I fed ocher leaves to the stream to see which ones would collect in the eddy of a small boulder and which ones would find the current that carried them further.

I watched so closely, I almost fell in, just so I wouldn't have to look at you or feel the bright, soft stab of sunlight echoing the cloudless sky on Bear Creek. The water was a reflection of the sky, the season, our hearts, our flowing frailties and our eternal cycles. The water was a moving mirror and I wanted to look, but I couldn't. I looked at everything else, just to avoid the reflection.

I continued to document the direction and frequency of bubbles, sticks and other debris just to delay the thoughts of us, of reality, and the inevitable current of the stream.

Nursing

Draining the drowsiness from you like the sun coming for the ice on the eaves. Drip, drip, dripping to collect in puddles on patches of grass that drink deep and stay green even in late December just outside your kitchen window.

I wipe the fog from the glass and you wince at the light that finds your winterized eyes, but you don't move. You hold your coffee like a crucifix and pray over the cream spiraling white and gold through the black-brown. I don't want to disturb you, I know what you've been going through so I place an oil pan under your chair and leave you alone at the table to let the puddles of weariness collect.

I'll come to empty the pan in an hour or two and make some more coffee.

And just so you know, there's nothing I wouldn't do for you if you asked.

Writers Make
Terrible Partners

The clouds stand poised above us like sumo wrestlers in leotards, bursting at the seams. I chuckle to myself and you ask why, but I can't just say, "Because leotard is a funny word." Of course you'd ask me to explain, and then I'd have to retrace the chaotic steps I took in my world of thoughts to come to such a statement. By that time the humor would have been lost, the simple joy of daydreaming would be gone. It just isn't worth it.

You say I keep things from you. I want to tell you that it's not true, but just like other times when I'm laughing or weeping in my mind I reply, "I'm crazy, you know this. It wouldn't work to explain it."

Don't frown like that, even though I love the ugly way it makes you more beautiful. Don't heave out such a heavy sigh and don't, please don't look away to the clouds out the window. It will make me giggle again.

And then you've had it. You turn on me like the sun on Mercury and I implore you not to scorch the messenger. But the loneliness, the distances I retreat to, the love affair I have with my imagination, all the times I have held you in the dark with my body while my spirit soared the astral realms. It all comes raining down on you just as the clouds erupt and it's too much, too much for me. I let loose with a belly laugh, thinking of gargantuan Asians in a ballet and a crowd being rained upon by stitches and sweat and saliva, but unable to look away.

You turn around, stare out the window at the rain, and when you return you're stained like the sky. I remember how much I hate myself for loving the way you look when you cry. But it's too late to explain away anything. You've picked up your coat and your keys, you tell me you're leaving, and you hope that some day I'll find someone who I can share my madness with. And the hardest part, you continue speaking so clearly through tears, the hardest part is that it's the insanity in me that you that most, even though it's what keeps me from you.

You have more to say but instead you turn away. A cold, electric tempest pours in as you open the door and when it closes I think to myself that the clouds and the rain are much more like the weather on Venus—brimstone, poisonous, caustic. But it's too late. I'll have to share my thoughts with paper and pen and wonder whether you were the ink or the blank page.

Entitled

There are too many leaves on the trees, too many clouds, not enough sun, or too much sun and it's melting my ice cream. I complain like it was my job as the supreme overseer and emperor of minimal details.

You rush outside, climb the tree outside our window and prune the leaves until I approve, though I'll probably send you back up tomorrow with some super glue.

You call in favors from the ocean and the moon, collecting debts that you will have to pay in the afterlife all so you can cover or open up the sky at my every wanton whim.

I'm not rich enough, nor famous, not appreciated, not deified. You section off pieces of your soul, sell it in installments to the devil just so I can get a few poems published.

I'm sad, anxious, angry, upset, or just plain petulant about any and every thing. You harness the western wind and hire a hot air balloon to follow the sunset across the earth until I've calmed down enough to smile at you.

It's not fair. What the sky gives so freely, what the earth grows so selflessly, and what you do just to keep me happy. I wouldn't wish that task on anybody. But somehow it falls on you.

I want you to know that I'm trying to warm my own bottle, to self-soothe, to forego the mountains out of molehills. I hope that you know that I notice all the things you do. I'm trying to learn from you. Because though you are limitless there's bound to be an end to how much entitlement one woman can put up with.

Boys Will Be

In the overgrown, ripening summer, four boys, elementary age, chase the day away. It is that magic hour, right after dinner, just before the dark comes and beds call. It is twilight when boys can claim ten-foot tall dirt mountains on construction sites as their own kingdom. It is that time of not-day, not-yet-night when shadows grow longer than they ever will get and when the sun casts mirages and mirrors on tin trash can lids and car windows.

It is this moment when Hector takes his playschool plastic three-wheeler into the alley behind his house to play games of bravery, rivalry and danger with his brother and cousins. They take turns at first, on the "Big Wheel" as Hector calls it. He is only slightly too big for it. His brother, Cameron, outgrew it last year and his cousins played on it when they were six, but even then they barely fit. Hector is small for his age, but he controls the group dynamic, and he knows it.

Simple turn-taking becomes poking and prodding, becomes challenges to intellect, ability and manhood. Hector's youngest cousin, Manny, takes the Big Wheel out of turn when Hector turns too fast and falls. While Hector still nurses a scraped knee, Manny lifts the Big Wheel above his head, like some tyrannical Cyclops. Hector screams, his most valued possession hurled like felled timber before the howling and jeers of his kin.

Something in Hector snaps, erupts like a hot, battered soda can and he leaps for Manny, fingers brandished like Wolverine's claws. He strikes Manny's face, narrowly missing his eyes. Fingernail scratches on Manny's temple will be attributed to a tree branch when their mothers ask later, but at this moment they are cause for retribution, for war.

The two boys roll and rage on the shark skin cement. Neither commit to full blows or all-out fist fighting, but the potential is there as their seething young muscles grapple. Cameron and Vinny, in their upper elementary wisdom, know instigation and co-conspiracy charges when they see them. They look at each other, wordless, and run for an alibi. Manny and Hector continue to tumble, teeth bared, neither acknowledging the inevitable truce they know they must come to.

For it is not this day, not this sunset when they will at last come to terms with their places in existence, in the hierarchy of boys that becomes the hierarchy of men that becomes the structure of civilization. It is not yet their time to accept their lots and play the cards they've been dealt.

During this dusk, all things are still possible. And so they curse each other more, but eventually let go. They examine their own wounds first and then the wounds of their adversary. And at this time, they can still feel the pain of the other. They can still regret the suffering caused. They can still walk away, holding each other up unsteadily and, together, tell their mothers a unified lie.

The Father, the Son

You are different today. Not the same as Wednesday when I came over for dinner. Not the same at all.

You say you wept like you haven't in who knows how long. You were thinking of him—the look on his face—in the waiting room of the oncology ward.

You wept so hard you woke up Mom, you couldn't help it. Just thinking of him waiting for his wife—the look on his face.

You couldn't say it, but it was there hanging like dark clouds. The question: what if it were you in the waiting room?

The question has changed you. Your edges have softened. Your eyes are deeper with pain, and love, and brighter with understanding. Today you speak easier on the way home down the winding mountain road. You speak of old things seen in a new light: addiction, mistakes, waste, the rage writhing inside. (I know it too, your blood is mine, remember?)

Dad, you make me proud. I'm not angry anymore, I'm not even sore. I don't know how, it just comes like dawn, like sunlight through clouds, like rain to the desert—all of these things that are out of my hands.

Old pain is not something you just forget. But the look on your face, the sound of your voice tells me we can all be forgiven.

May we all forgive this dream.

The Worst Day of My Life

So there I was coming down Navajo. I had just picked up Ms. Holloway at 36th, she gave me her usual shy, coquettish (at least in my mind) smile. I said something especially charming that made her laugh. I was thinking to myself that today could be the day I finally ask her out for coffee and pie. Do people still do that? I've been out of the game for too long. Ms. Holloway probably has too. She still wears her wedding ring, even though she's been a widow for 6, 7 years.

I was coming up on the 34th street stop and Kim was waiting for me. The guy had been riding my route for years and all I knew about him was his name, Kim. I didn't even know if it was his last name or his first. Anyways, I was probably thinking about Ms. Holloway a little too much, about how I might suggest a date when she was getting off at her stop. Should I hand her a transfer and hold her hand for just a second? Should I mention what time my shift is done? I hadn't felt that light and giddy in years. Like a kid again, and wouldn't you know it, I take a corner too sharp. Bam!

Well, it was more like a slow screech of metal on metal and a dim thud, but I knew I was in deep. Right at that moment I felt like Muhammad Ali had punched me a good one in the gut. I wanted to puke. This was my third incident in less than 8 months. It would be grounds for termination. It all started with that crazy hobo, who jumped in front of my bus. Nothing I could've done. The guy was cooked out of his mind, couldn't tell up from down. I didn't hurt him too bad. I explained, the boss understood, but he had to write me up anyway. Then there was biker, didn't put his bike on the rack right. It fell off, I ran it over. It was his fault, but I was supposed to have noticed the improper loading. Strike two.

And now here I was, talking to the police and the RTD incident reporters. It was nothing, just a little dent in the fender, but it would cost me my job. They wouldn't care that I've been doing this for thirty years. Gabriel, my supervisor, the little prick, half my age and never really worked a day in his life. Sitting behind his desk, he doesn't know anything about being behind the wheel. But the worst part, Ms. Holloway, she'd have to walk. That's what really killed me. And I didn't even get to say goodbye. The only good thing about the day was taking the longest smoke break I've had in years.

Unrequited Love of the Self

From the brain to the heart:
Do you find me assuming, needy or unbearably aloof? Am I a good listener, or do I talk too much? Are my subjects relevant to you? I know how I look like fat, slimy, senile worms burrowing into each other, like an upside down bowl of wrinkled linguine suspended in amniotic jello. I wouldn't be attracted to me, but since it's you, and you are the way you are. Well, just check the box for yes, no or maybe.

From central nervous system to feet:
Don't think I haven't noticed you. You and your down-trodden elegance. You and your articulate curves. Your electric, delicate lines that bear the weight of the world, that lift the soul and dance the very breath of this body's corporeal connection. In every step you make I feel your care, your consideration, your staggering love. I know how much my supple spine owes to your grace, your tender strength. My dear, will you offer me the sweet satisfaction of one night: you, me, and a delicious soak in epsom salts? I won't beg, and I won't push, but my darling you must know that I burn for you.

From the rectum to the mouth:
I know we're supposed to be on opposite ends of the spectrum, but, well, just tell me if I'm way off base. I just, well, I feel like you've been giving me signals lately. I've noticed that the food the last few weeks is so thoughtfully

chewed. My secretions of late are nothing short of miracles, and it's all thanks to you. I think you are my muse. I know how this sounds, I'm sure I'm the last thing your lips would want to kiss, and I've a tendency to make an ass of myself. But I thought I'd throw caution to the broken wind, and, anyways, anything is possible right? It can't hurt to just ask. You know where to find me.

Life Lessons of the Periodic Table

Bryan and I should have decided much earlier on that it was in our best interest and in the interest of the preservation of the world at large to not hang out. Some elements, when combined with other elements just have a way of exploding or corroding or poisoning or causing lesions. It's the way of nature. Hydrogen, for example, is essential to so many necessities of life, but it's highly flammable, and when combined with sulfur and oxygen it makes sulfuric acid.

But other elements are just plain nasty alone or merged, like fluorine, mercury, arsenic. I don't know whether Bryan and I were like the more harmless, inert elements and we just created the wrong kind of reaction, or if we were the toxic elements and we just multiplied our deadly effects. At that time of our lives, in our unstable, highly reactive teens, I would lean toward the latter.

The first strike was a pocketknife to the throat. It was a direct hit, small, pointy end first, but it barely left a scratch on my throat. It wasn't Bryan that flicked the knife, but he was in the room and I think our rudiments had already started intermingling. Landon had dealt the near fatal wrist flick as he was trying to open a small knife "like they do in the movies." But Landon and I were just like any other two ignorant, self-destructive elements on the periodic table, licentious but not lethal. Though he had been the one who first introduced me to the lady Mary Jane, and he was in the passenger seat when I broke the axle of my Pontiac Grand

Am doing donuts on our lunch break, I don't think it was his noxious nuances guiding the knife.

The second strike came later on, the same day as the misfired pocketknife. Landon, Bryan and I had a jovial afternoon of violence shooting each other with small balls full of paint, propelled at vicious, stinging speeds. Bryan had a house in a then undeveloped area where there was plenty of open prairie, small ravines and boulders to have a great time playing war games.

The game was done. We wore our welts and bruises with pride. Protective masks were off and we were all ready to call it a day. But not before I got one last shot in. I was walking toward Landon and Bryan from my side of a small growth of trees. I was perhaps a hundred yards away, a very long distance, a distance that most paintballers would not expect to hit even a large target, let alone a bull's-eye.

I lifted up my gun in jest. I called Bryan's name from afar. He looked up and I took careless aim and fired. The paintball was not meant to come anywhere near Bryan's person, perhaps within a few feet at best. Just a final, wisecracking shot we could laugh about later when we recounted all the great plays of the game. But it hit its target. It was so accurate in fact that Billy the Kid would have likened it to shooting a fly right between its wings. Bryan went down.

My little joke, our amusing day, my stomach all went sinking down to the bottom of the Marianas Trench. I ran over to Bryan with a feeling of abysmal dread. He was holding his face and groaning in distress. Lance was crouched down next to him asking if he was all right, but getting no response through the moaning and doom in the air. Our parents would never let us play with paintball guns again.

We got Bryan to a hose and helped him wash out his eye. I couldn't tell if it was blood or paint in his eye. We rinsed it off, it was blood. Bryan's eye had become a bulging, scarlet orb, a horrific contusion. He couldn't see through it at all. I almost threw up, thinking that I had blinded him. We took him inside and after he was in a somewhat stable condition we confirmed the lie that we would tell his mother. I left in shame and shambles. I couldn't even take pride in the shot of a lifetime. Bryan's sight returned later on that same day, but he still has little to no depth perception and probably won't for life, all from one wicked shot that should never have made its mark.

Bryan and I didn't consciously choose to not hang out after that, but I think we both understood there was something dangerous about our alliance. We steered clear of close, prolonged contact for a while after that. But a year or so later, after the optical wound had healed, we decided to go up for a day to snowboard. The day went great. No one came to any near death conclusions during our high speed game of tag in the trees. Neither of us broke anything as we risked life and limb jumping 10, 20 high off jumps in the terrain park. Even the rails proved bloodless.

It was on our way back that the third strike struck. Bryan was driving his small Honda Civic. It had snowed earlier in the day, but the sun was shining on our triumphant return home. There was a bit of slush and snow on I-70, but it was nothing we hadn't driven on a thousand times in Colorado. Bryan was passing people in the left lane at 70 or 75 m.p.h. All of a sudden the car started to turn. I assumed Bryan was just changing lanes. But then the car started to turn more. I looked over at Bryan and his mouth was open in a soundless "Oh shit!" I knew something was wrong. We continued to turn and turn until we were rotated 180 degrees.

We screamed and wailed in unison. The traffic was now coming directly for us like the bulls of Pamplona. Except these bulls were made of metal, filled with combustible liquids and traveling between 60 and 75 m.p.h. We had no time to say our prayers or recount the deeds of our life, both righteous and wicked. There was only time to scream and spin and hope for a quick end.

But the car continued its trajectory and rotated a full 360 degrees. We came crashing into a snow bank on the shoulder and stopped dead in our frictionless tracks. The car stalled, we stepped out like hostages from a plane expecting to have to be towed home. But there was not a mark on the car that we could see. When we got back in after jumping and shouting and praising the names of our numberless gods and guardian angels, the car started with only a hesitant whine. We drove home a bit slower, with a little more reverence for life. We never spent time together one on one again.

I imagine that each of us has a thin thread of life that the Fates hold in their hands and fray or singe or gnaw on continuously until they snap. I don't know what my thread is made of, or Bryan's; it's either some thin, but indestructible metal like Wolverine's adamantium skeleton or its some rare unearthly silly putty with properties like flubber. Whatever it is that we are composed of, life and near-death showed us that some elements should not be combined.

Foregone Conclusion

He counted up thirty-five dollars and 76 cents, not a bad haul for a half day's work. He decided to call it a day then, stashed his cardboard sign in the bush next to his corner. It was his lucky corner, he had fought hard for it. The Colonel had picked it out, deciding it was strategically the most valuable corner in the square mile radius. He listened to the Colonel, even though Suzy said it was too loud and dirty. He quieted Suzy with a promise that he would buy her candy. That always worked with Suzy.

He found his way to the river path through brambles and thick bushes filled with garbage, glass and needles. He went to his favorite thinking spot. It was under the cool shade of a bridge, right on the bank of the river where an overhanging grassy patch reached out and called his name. It didn't call his name like the voices, he knew the difference. It just beckoned to him, and he obeyed.

Now it was time to sit and think about what to make of the money. He could go get a warm meal, he hadn't eaten what could be considered a true meal in several days. He could buy a bottle of something, he hated the taste, but when he had a bottle he had friends, though he would have to share. He could rent a bed for the night. A good nights sleep, a shower, and a shave would certainly not hurt. But he already knew what he was going to do with the money. It had already been decided, though the debate had raged between the voices for weeks. He was going to buy a present for Suzy.

It was not the shrill, scared Suzy that spoke to him when it got dark or strangers threatened him. It was the real Suzy, he knew the difference. She was around 12 now, sometimes he would go far out of his normal path, even though the voices would scream at him telling him he was going too far. He would go to see Suzy while she walked home from school. She never saw him, he made sure of that, he wanted to keep her safe. He knew it was his duty to protect her. He knew it from the time before, though he could not remember much more.

He got up from his thinking spot by the river and went to the grocery store. They didn't like him there, so he let Georgie do the talking. He would ask for candy and toys, maybe a squirt gun, and some beef jerky for himself. He rehearsed with Georgie before he went in. When he walked in the security guard started to push him out, but when he shouted and held up his money the nice manager man with the soft face and big black eyes let him shop. He just said to make it quick.

He took the river path and then walked away from his habitual home one step at a time. The voices did not scream as loud this time, probably because they had debated for so long before the decision had been made. He was glad.

He walked with his bag of presents through the city. It was a long walk for him on shoes with soles worn so thin his feet ached and bled. But he had to see Suzy, he had to give her her presents and he had to tell her something. What was it? He could not remember now. He tried and tried the whole walk to remember what was so important that he had to tell her. As he walked he fought past hordes of pigeons who wished to take his presents for their own. He forced his way through crowds of people who, with their eyes, tried to take his thoughts from him and steal Suzy's image from his mind. But he prevailed. He found himself in the alley across from Suzy's school just as the bell rung.

And there she was. It was her. He knew it was her. He walked toward her. He stopped. The voices that had been in agreement before, undammed their agreements and a cacophony let loose inside his head. They screamed and smashed against each other, he fell to his knees, tears streaming down his face. He wanted this, but his voice was lost among the swelling sea of voices in his head. He crawled toward Suzy, though the voices pushed him down. He tore his pants, blood streamed from his knees. He was so close.

He was almost to Suzy and her group of friends. They had their backs to him and had not noticed him yet. He was so close. He reached out his hand with the bag of presents. He was so close. And then he felt his arm in the grasp of a strong hand. His other arm was pulled behind him. Words were spoken, but he could not hear them over the voices. His arms were in handcuffs. He was carried to a police car. He saw Suzy, her mother holding her frantically. Her mother was crying, buckets of tears. She looked at him. He knew her, though the voices told him he didn't. He looked at Suzy, fear and confusion in her eyes. He pleaded with his eyes to the fallen bag at her feet. She looked at it. She looked back at him. She looked at her mother who was busy talking to the police. Suzy picked up the bag and smiled. She waved at him. He lay back in his seat and waves of relief washed over him.

The voices could shout all they wanted. He was at peace.

Buick LeSabre

1991, it was their first new car as a young couple. Silently ecstatic as they took it off the lot, both feeling the same dual sense of joy and dread as they drove off. Was it really theirs? Could they really afford this? It had been no hasty decision. At least six months of shopping around, reading consumer reviews, talking to mechanics. But still, now that the moment had finally arrived, they felt like children taking home a shining new toy. A toy that they would be paying off for the next 10 years.

Bruce washed and detailed it every weekend; Jan drove it like it was fine china on wheels, with a V6. They wouldn't let the kids eat in the car, not on the leather seats. Some balmy summer nights they would sit on the porch, sipping iced tea and marveling at the champagne colored sedan, shimmering like a mirage in the setting sun.

The first time the Buick saw hail, they held each other, watching helplessly from the window. Bruce had moved it under a tree, it was the best they could do without a garage. They cringed as golf ball sized comets fell like a plague upon their pride and joy. Their children cried in fear as thunder and hail pounded down, but there was no comfort for anyone that day.

Years passed and time, in its slow, unnoticeable way, ravished the Buick, along with children and their ice cream cones, spilt cokes, windows left down in the rain. Bruce washed the car only when it was too dirty to see out of. Jan hit the brakes a little harder, was less kind to the engine as she accelerated. They no longer sat on the porch with iced tea. They paid less attention to the car, less attention to each other. It was around the car's 10th birthday and their 15th anniversary that the front windows started acting up. First the passenger side, and then the driver's, until one day both windows got stuck halfway and they never rolled up or down again.

It was an ugly divorce. She took the house and the kids; he got the car and hefty alimony payments. Bruce sold the LeSabre to a high school kid named Jason for $1,200. His hand was shaking when he signed over the title, Bruce almost hugged Jason when he handed him the keys. He turned and walked the mile back to his apartment looking at every car that passed like it might be his Buick returning, brand new, born again, carrying the life he had lost in its roomy seats.

Jason didn't mind the windows. He solved that problem with clear packaging tape, which he replaced every month or two when the tape got too murky to see through. He covered the cracked leather seats with thrift store afghans and pasted the bumper with stickers of his favorite bands. As a final act of both style and rebellion, he had his brother help him fasten a snowboard to the trunk. The snowboard, secured with screws and metal brackets, acted as a spoiler. Jason took special pride in parking his car next to the rich kids' new sports cars with real spoilers in his high school parking lot.

The Buick became the refuge for a tight group of friends who passed their days and nights in parks, baseball dugouts, parking lots, or wherever they found themselves that was away from parents or guardians. It could not be said that the LeSabre was treated with care or respect, but it was used, valued, and became something of a second home to Jason for his high school career. A home that was often times more safe and comforting than his first home.

Though the sedan became cluttered with trash, choked with smoke and teenage funk, it was a haven for the 10 or so rotating friends who roamed the suburban streets thick as thieves. Jason took it in for regular oil changes, if nothing else, and installed a new CD player, which pushed thick, guttural screams and heavy distortion through struggling speakers for the whole neighborhood to hear.

It was the summer between junior and senior year that Jason lost his virginity in the Buick. It was the last week before school began, his friend had been having a week-long party while his parents were out of town. Jason would never forget that sweaty, blurry night or the fundamental act on the musty afghans, all two minutes of it.

When Jason moved from the suburbs to the city for college, he decided a bicycle would suffice for all his transportation needs. He had his own apartment now and it was no longer necessary to have a mobile safe house from his parents. With great regret and lament, he removed the afghans from the seats and sang a silent funeral dirge as he placed them in the dumpster. He put the Buick on craigslist, and sold it for $600 the next day.

When Jason signed over the title he wrote down the current mileage of the car: 117,567. He had bought it at 67, 384 miles. That was 50,000 miles he had spent with this automobile. A couple about his age from the mountains had taken it gladly, but they did not seem as happy about the car as they were about the price. They closed the doors a little too hard and turned the ignition a little too long. He watched the car drive down the street and turn the block and he had a vision of the future.

He knew that many years from then, he would look back at this day and see himself on that street corner watching his car drive away. And he knew that that moment would be dog-eared, like a well-read page in a book, which he would revisit again and again as he reviewed his life's plot.

The Creek

I remember the last days of the crawdad wars. That was the story we told each other when we couldn't find a living thing anywhere swimming in the creek. Though it wasn't a war at all; it was a massacre, a genocide. We used to live and breathe that creek. It was our sanctuary. And as kids, we worshipped in the holiest, most honest ways. We took our shoes off to wade in the mud-luscious holy water. We did our best to get lost in cattail labyrinths and caught minnows, snakes, skinks, seeing how long we could keep them alive in glass jars.

The dirt hills were the first to go. My brothers taught me how to ride those rollers. They showed me how to hit a jump at full speed, how to land, and how to take a fall. I can still see them on those battered bikes, soaring ten feet, twenty, I swear, we all saw it. But they flattened those dirt hills before I had the chance to jump the gap that all the big kids said I was too small for, I'd die if I tried. It seemed like they were there one day, and the next, a strip mall, asphalt, concrete paving over our childhood.

The creek remained. I think it's still there, a protected reserve. But nothing lives there now, not a crawdad, not a salamander, nothing but spiders. The creek still runs, but it's dead, choked with pollution; it's black and blue like a bruise. In that slow, golden blaze of childhood, the sun sets so gradually you never notice until it's pitch black all of a sudden. That's how it was with the creek.

One day we were playing in the muck-lovely water, seeing how close we could get our fingers to the crawdads' pinchers.

And then all of a sudden night came to the creek, everything died, or disappeared, or wilted.

The sun never rose again.

Welcome Back

The shoots of green grass, it's time. Put away the scarf, the snow shovel, and come back to us.

You've spent the last season with moon, with dreams, with stillness sitting inside, traveling many distances. We understand your silence, and if you wish to speak, we'll listen. But all we really need is your company.

It's OK, your eyes will adjust. It's OK if you fall asleep, if you're awkward, if you're not in the best mood. All we really want is you.

Here, have some tea, beer, wine? Hungry? You must be after what you've been through.

ON MIND, BODY, HEART AND SOUL

Coyote's Last Days

There was a knock on the door and Genevieve sighed heavily. It was 8 a.m., which meant it could only be one of two people. Her girlfriend, just stopping by to surprise her on the way to work. Which only happened once, back when they were first dating, one year and 3 months ago, and had not happened since. Or it would be…

"Mr. Latrans, what a surprise," Genevieve already had the cream in her hand, ready to fill his empty cup.

"It seems that I have mistaken my…" He looked surprised as Genevieve topped him off, but did not even attempt to finish his sentence.

Most of the time he just stood there silent, staring blankly at the cup before stuttering steps took him back to his apartment. But every once in a while he looked up with a dull, but decidedly devilish gleam in his eye. It was for this gleam that Genevieve still answered the door 1-5 days a week at 8 a.m. Because with this gleam came stories.

"Back in my day, you could still read clouds. Like, actually read them, like a book or a tweet, whatever it is you punks actually read. I don't know, you kids are into some crazy stuff now. But you can't read the clouds. And because of this, the clouds have stopped speaking. Every once in a while I get a little whisper of something, but it's not much. Just a 'nice weather we're having…' or something stupid like that."

He scratched himself, or tried to like he was still not used to his body. His foot reached for his side, but after his knee surgery and his steel hip, the foot didn't move more than a couple inches off the ground.

He was talking, but not the good stuff. Not the things that Genevieve could use to feed her muse. She had deadlines and couldn't waste time on false leads.

"OK Mr. Latrans, look, I've really gotta—"

"And another thing." He could not scratch himself so he chewed on his right forearm with the 12 teeth left in his head. "There used to be a dance. Once a month, or at the very least, every 13th moon too."

"Oh?" Genevieve perked up a bit.

"Oh yes," he answered hoarsely. "A dance that made the moon bloom like a poppy and brought the stars to falling like it was raining light. You kids and your clubs. You wouldn't know a damn thing about real dancing."

"You've been to a lot of clubs then?" Genevieve teased him.

He frowned, but she knew he liked her banter.

"A few, pshhh," he waved her off, "practically invented clubs, and the whole party scene. That was when being irreverent actually meant something. You kids, now everyone pees on the fire. Everybody's a God damning goddamn trickster."

He was winding up, Genevieve liked that. He was beginning to shuffle in his stance just a bit, and chew on his tongue. She recognized these signs. He looked at her and winked. She felt her heart leap ever so slightly. His winks, when they came, were either total duds or they went off like a wet firework. Genevieve was absolutely certain that when he was younger, Mr. Latrans's winks had the coercive effects of a shotgun blast to all those in the vicinity.

"I've got something for you," he said.

His gaze was now a little too bright. Mr. Latrans looked to Genevieve's robe, and then down to her bare feet. He licked his lips, absently. It made a dry, dead leaf sound.

"I've got everything I need, thanks." Genevieve had an automatic response to creeps, pervs and other desperate catcalls.

"Oh, I seriously doubt that."

He looked for a hesitant moment like another person, another creature entirely. But then he was back, a mothball-mouthed old man with gray hair sprouting from the back and sides of his head like tufts of wild animal fur. He smiled slyly for a second and then he reached into his mouth. He coughed and gagged, drool puddled down at his feet and on his crusty pajamas. Genevieve was about to reach out and yank his hand away, as you would a baby. But then Mr. Latrans extracted his hand, all glistening with saliva and blood.

Genevieve was appalled to the point of frozen stupor. She wanted to recoil as Latrans reached for her hand, but some petrifying revulsion kept her immobile. He opened her hand and placed in the palm a long, bloody tooth. Then he closed her hand again.

"Just shhomething to remember me by," his speech was slurred by the blood in his mouth and the one less tooth he now talked through.

"I, I, don't—" Genevieve stammered.

"Jussht wasssh it off. Keep it shomewhere shafe. Bessht if it were necssht to some antlersh or in a shpider shilk cashe. There'sh power in that toosh. And there'sh medicine in foolishnesh. Don't go forgetting me now."

He turned to waddle off, but then turned back.

"Oh yea, Shanks for the cream."

He excused himself and Genevieve dreamily walked back to the couch in her apartment, forgetting to close the door.

She opened up her hand and through the viscous saliva and blood she examined the tooth. It was long and pointed, brown and yellow. It was at least as long as half her pinky. There was no way this had come from Mr. Latrans's mouth. Nonetheless, as she held it, she felt a leaping, laughing, recklessly abandoning electricity course through her. She almost joined in when she heard the howl from down the hall. It was actually a half-howl, half-screaming yip and it made her shiver to her bones, but it did not frighten her.

Waking Life

What a way to wake, with a cold shoulder, uncovered, kissing her ear and a too-hot chest pressing into the mattress. A sunbeam purrs beside her, the smell of gray clouds and snow on an apple-crisp winter morning. And for the sweetest of seconds she forgot she woke alone, she forgot she woke. She forgot about being here in the world or rented rooms. She nearly forgot that there was anywhere outside of dreams.

I Sing the Body Neglected

At the end of the day, half-empty beer can resting on the stomach, suspended in viscera, framed by bone and nourished by blood. All kept together autonomously in a self-contained cosmos.

"What a day!"

You scratch your crotch like itching was your job.

We all seek support, sex, money, validation, and relief from the numberless neuroses we create from dust. We demand satisfaction and superfluous commodities like luxury was our birthright. But the body, oh the body, asks for so little. Just some measly crumbs, dew drops from an olive leaf, rest on something softer than a rock. And what do we give back to our mind and soul's vehicle while it burns the calories on both ends?

A weekend binge, an energy drink, an occasional spin class and arms that can't even reach to scratch your own back.

Corpus Corvidae

The rising sun bleeds in through the curtains. You try to bandage the light on your eyes with your pillow and return to dreams of losing your teeth or using the toilet in the middle of a mall. Then comes a crow outside your window. He's left his murder to caw a capella in that screeching, grating, baby strangling voice that makes you wonder what God or Nature, or evolution were thinking. They are all equally irresponsible. It makes you believe that some things in life are just meant to be ugly, trying, enraging.

This is not the way you wanted to start your day, with thoughts of killing another being. You emerge from bed, begrudgingly, with some big questions. Crows are supposed to be highly intelligent, why, then, do they sound like idiots? You prefer ravens, is that just because of Poe or anthropomorphic associations? Supposedly, a parliament of rooks will gather, encircle one rook and after much cawing and cacophony peck the lone rook to death. Is it because the rook was sick or breeding diseases? Or was the rook saying something the other members of the parliament disagreed with?

Either way, the day begins with or without you and this whole corvidae business reminds you of a joke: What's the difference between a crow and a raven? Raven's have one more feather on the wings than crows. These feathers, used for flight, are called pinions. So, really, it's just a matter of a pinion.

Angels

With three shoppers in the checkout line ahead of her at Wal-Mart, Belle browsed through the magazines. Deciding upon *People Magazine*, she opened to an article on Brittany Spears.

To no one in particular she exclaimed: "Oh, that hussy, she should be ashamed of herself. I can't believe they're letting her come back."

A few shoppers snuck quick, concerned glances at her, but no one responded to Belle's statement. She put the magazine back on the rack, not being gentle as she forced it into line with the others of its kind. Her short, shallow breathing, her red face, and her dragon-like huffs and puffs alarmed the customers nearby. She turned her attention to her shopping cart and took inventory of her groceries.

One at a time she placed each item onto the conveyor belt. One box of aluminum foil, one box of plastic wrap. Her breathing had normalized more now and her face was less flushed. One package of instant oats. She deliberated for a moment with a furrowed brow, then removed the oats, placed them back in her cart and selected instead scented garbage bags next. She continued placing her items in an orderly fashion at a steady pace that one could set a metronome to. Now the instant oats, next the bag of assorted frozen vegetables, then, still one at a time, but stacked perfectly on top of each other, five frozen pizzas—meat lovers, followed by one can of instant coffee, one box of Maxi pads—extra heavy, one jar of reduced fat peanut butter, one loaf of white bread, one jar of sugar free grape jelly, one gallon of skim milk, a 10 pound bag of cat food, and finally a package of baloney.

"Hello Ms. McKay," Donna, the cashier, said with a bright smile. "Looks like the usual for you today."

Belle turned her back to Donna and perused the candy and gum. Her arm reached out but then, as if slapped by an unseen disciplinary hand, Belle rapidly retracted it. She reached out once more, this time very slowly and warily she selected a nutrageous bar. Like all the other items she placed it in line, equally spaced from the item in front of it.

"Did you find everything all right today, Ms. McKay?" Donna asked with the same patient smile.

Belle muttered something just soft enough and just garbled enough to be unintelligible. She did not look at Donna. She opened her bright pink purse to retrieve her bright red wallet.

"Your total is going to be..." Donna paused, anticipating Belle's next move. Belle reached for *People Magazine* and placed it at the end of the line.

"OK, your total is now $53.08."

Belle counted out the exact change as Donna finished bagging the groceries. Donna took the money and waited for Belle to ask for two receipts. Donna then handed Belle the receipts and the extra plastic bags she always asked for.

"Have a good day, Ms. McKay."

Donna and the other shoppers watched Belle walk away without acknowledgment and head to the 50-cent extra large gumball machine.

Belle placed the gumball in her purse and then walked out the doors to the bus stop. A young child passed her by and stared. His mother dragged him along even as his head rotated 180 degrees to continue staring after Belle. He stopped walking, he kept craning his neck to look after Belle.

"Come on, Mikey! I got shit to do. Get your ass up or I'm just gonna drag you."

"But, but," Mikey pleaded, "didn't you see that lady?"

"Yea I saw her. It ain't polite to stare, boy. You know that. Now come on. I ain't carrying you."

"You didn't see them things?"

"What things? Shit, you better not be going blind. I can't afford no glasses for you."

His mother was fed up and took to dragging him again. All the customers in line stared, but she did not care. Let them try and raise four kids by themselves, see how they liked it. She got a cart, and tossed Mikey in.

"I saw them," he went on. His mother ignored him. "I saw them, I swear. They were flying above her, a bunch of 'em. Angels."

An elderly lady, wearing her curlers, had walked in just behind Mikey and his mother. She was waiting patiently to grab a cart. She smelled like stale cigarettes and the two red beers she had had for breakfast. Her teeth were yellow, and her face was as wrinkled as a pile of dirty laundry. Mikey liked her, he smiled, talking to her now since he knew his mother wasn't listening.

"I saw 'em. They were right there. Floating all around her. I think there were 10, maybe 200 of them. All bright and shiny. Did you see them?"

"Mikey! Quiet, now! Don't be bothering people with your stories. No one wants to hear them. If you keep telling lies you gonna get a whooping. Better watch out."

Mikey knew his mother's threats were not empty. He continued to plead with the old lady with his eyes. She smiled and nodded. She put her finger to her mouth and then pointed up above her. Mikey looked up and saw angels.

Rapture

"Come on in, dear. Sit down," Dwight's mother indicated the teal vinyl couch.

Dwight's stomach knotted up. At 28, an adult is not supposed to fear invitations to "talk" with one's parents. But Dwight's mother, Deana, and father, Dale, always had a way of making him feel like he had done something naughty that his face needed rubbing in.

"Well, son," Dale began once they were all uncomfortably seated in the family room. "Now, we've gotten the house appraised recently and your mother and I have been saving up, hiding our nuts, if you will."

Dwight had a sudden impulse to tell his dad why nut references were not appropriate, but he held back. He knew it was best to just bite the bullet and let his parents say whatever they felt needed saying.

Dale sighed and looked at Deana, already exasperated. Dwight's mother took over.

"What your father means to say," she chirped, "is that we have some savings put away. We don't trust the banks, Obama and those socialists are going to take over any day now. So, we—we have some money hidden in the house."

She smiled. It was the same smile she used when she told the Mormons who came knocking on the door that Jesus still loved them.

"Now, Dwight." Dale was ready to get to the real heart of the matter. Dwight saw it in the way he fiddled absentmindedly with his comb-over. "You see, son, well, the thing is..."

He was having a hard time getting it out, whatever it was. He looked pleadingly at Deana.

"What your father is trying to say. Is that Jesus is coming soon."

Dale looked lovingly at his faithful wife. He squeezed her knee.

"That's right," he pulled nervously on the hair of his earlobes, "He is coming. Soon. Too many prophecies have been fulfilled. The temple is being rebuilt. The beast has been born. It's happening. Sooner than we think. This September, actually."

Dale looked at Deana for support, which he knew he could always count on. Dwight's jaw hung slack, he was in utter disbelief.

"Yes." Deana continued driving the derailed train, "September. The rapture will come first, of course. And then, well, Dwight dear, I'm afraid it won't be very pleasant for you and the other unbelievers during the end times."

Dwight didn't know whether to laugh or weep. He didn't know if he should try to explain how insane his parents' rationale was, or just smile and nod.

"Unpleasant," Dwight's father snuffed, "it will be Hell on earth! Demons unleashed, plagues, famine, the Four Horsemen of the Apocalypse will reign supreme and the beast will brand everyone with his mark. Dwight—we wish—we just wanted so much more for you. The Kingdom of Heaven could have been yours."

"What your father means, Dwight," Deana stepped in, as if she could salvage this wreck of a family talk, "is that there's still time to repent. But not much. And well, we don't need to go into all that now. So all we really wanted to tell you is that there's money in the house."

"Yes," Dale continued, "we'll leave a note on the kitchen table with all the details. When the rapture comes and you're still—well—here. At least we will know that we left you with something."

Dwight's mother and father were holding hands, looking at Dwight with pity, as only the righteous can look upon the damned. A thousand curses, arguments, and logical fallacies were racing through his mind. There were so many things he wanted to say, so many ways to express his anger, pain, disbelief and sadness.

Dwight stood up. He drew in a deep, hissing breath.

"Well," Dwight fought hard to keep his voice calm, "I'll see you in a month and then you can apologize for being such self-righteous assholes."

Deana and Dale just stared, speechless. All their fears had been verified.

"You can have your rapture," Dwight continued, "I'll take my chances with this life."

He walked toward the door.

"Oh, by the way, when you're still here in September, do I still get the money?"

Dwight laughed, dryly, all the way out of the house, but the laughter had soured before he opened his car door.

Trophy

*Don't get excited, don't shout, don't even smile, they don't
know what they have.* He had to tell himself these things to
keep his emotions under control. He had been looking for
this for twenty-five years, it was the final piece.

Dale Steinberg, 47, of Denver, Colorado had stumbled
upon a treasure at the ARC thrift store. It was $2.99, and it
was half off because orange tags were on sale. He wanted to
run out the door before anyone had the chance to recognize
what he had. But he forced himself to casually stroll to the
cash register, to look the cashier in the eye, ask how her day
was and exchange the dollar and sixty-two cents for the
completion of his life's work.

He walked out of the thrift store with hands trembling.
Dale spent over a minute trying to unlock his car door.
When he finally got in, doors closed, windows up, his
treasure beside him in the passenger seat, he let out a sigh
that shook the fuzzy dice hanging from his rearview mirror.
And then he wept. After the tears stopped streaming from
his eyes, he laughed like a lunatic, slapped the steering
wheel, whooped, hollered and cried again.

He looked over at the gleaming thing beside him. It was
only six inches high, made mostly of plastic, with gold
painted eagles, and a soccer ball embellished the top. It was
his now, his treasure, his trophy. Even though it said the
name David Hendrick, and it was a trophy for this boy's
1994 little league soccer season with the Boomers.

He picked it up, he cradled it in his arms. The whole
drive back to his studio apartment he sang along to classic
rock on the radio as though he were singing hymns to the

plastic trophy. When he arrived home he left his keys in the door, left the door open and ran to the mantle above the crumbling bricks that sealed up the decrepit fireplace.

The mantle was littered with other trinkets and knick-knacks, porcelain cats, sad clown figurines, fake flowers, and countless other baubles and doodads. He struggled for a moment finding the exact right position for the trophy, shifting other things around to get the placement just right. Dale placed the trophy in between the magic eight ball, and the Coca-Cola Santa Claus. Then he stepped back, gleamed with pride, his chest swelled with satisfaction.

Slowly, almost imperceptibly the living room glowed with an eerie blue-green light. The whole apartment vibrated until a low humming sound filled Dale and every object in the room with a sound like the primordial *om*.

"They're here," Dale wept.

He fell to his knees, arms upraised, waiting for deliverance.

The Heart's Back Door

If you somehow navigate the wilderness of pining trees, and escape the ever-hungry jaws of the desire wolves, you may, at last, come upon it, the often-overlooked entrance into Love. Where the bug zapper buzzes and burns and the fluorescent green porch light sings like a pale, sickly beacon to all who may journey the roads less lovely, and less travelled.

The screen door is flapping in the wind, teetering on its hinges. There is a bag of trash, meant to be taken to the dumpster eons ago. There is an empty milk crate, a single muddy boot, a bent fishing pole, a rusted suit of armor.

Go around the front and the door is virgin redwood, with ancient, Atlantian woodworking inlaid with ivory unicorn horns, adorned in gems, with a knocker of solid gold and a diamond peephole (if you ever get that close) that works backwards, revealing the vast cosmos inside.

But those who wait at the back door don't know about the front door, or if they do, they assume they aren't worthy. Just as those at the front don't know about the back, or if they do, they wouldn't stoop to walk around and touch less than holy ground.

Out back and out front and in every direction, endlessly, there are camps set up, shanty towns, cities, megalopolises and world-wide slums that spread for thousands of miles. Literally everyone in existence is gathered around this place that—in comparison to the billions seeking entrance—is as impenetrable as the eye of a needle, as exclusive as history's prophet and guru guest list. While they wait, they war and they shape, they die and they procreate, they condemn and bicker and battle and, at best, agree to disagree about the nature of Love and the name of the heart's owner. But most of all, they argue incessantly about the best way to enter in to Love.

Nonetheless, either entrance is as likely to open as the other for the one who, unassumingly, knocks and knows that all rooms in the house are one and the same, equally empty, equally infinite. Just as all entrances are uniformly arbitrary when we are all already inside.

The Mind

I was having brunch with my demons when my Shadow showed up uninvited, turning our pity party into a mid-morning massacre. I would have stayed in my hole wallowing, but then the synaptic mailman came at noon to deliver a letter from Rationality that read: "There are a thousand sides to every story, so please, step outside for a minute, or at least open a window."

So I took a walk to Mercy's apartment. She was out on an errand, but somehow she knew I'd be by. She left a note: "Yes, it's all in your head, but that doesn't make it any less real. Go see Compassion, she can help."

I took the train to the Upper Heart District and found her in a dive bar sipping ginger ale listening to every barfly's woeful tale. I asked for her advice and she shrugged: "Everyone's got problems. It's mostly a matter of how well you can love despite, or because of them."

She sent me next door to Pain who was lying on the linoleum, needle in his arm. I had to slap him awake. He didn't seem to mind but all I could get from his fevered fits was his mantra: "The cure is in me. The cure is in the pain." Then Blame came in, pushed me aside and told Pain he had to leave if he didn't have the rent.

I was utterly confused, no better or worse than before. I was ready to get a drink at Delusion's or rent a room for eternity at Oblivion's when a raven called to me from a streetlight.

"Say, I think I'm lost. I could use some directions."

"Couldn't we all?" was all I said.

"You look like you know the neighborhood," the raven said.

"I should. I created it."

"Well then, you must be why I'm here. Sometimes I get called in when there's a situation."

My face was a question. The raven answered:

"I'm from the realm of myth and archetypes. It looks like you could use some perspective. There's more to this world than what you make. 'Your mind is a place in and of itself,' but it's only one small world in an infinite cosmic sea. If you can't find Happiness and Peace eludes you perhaps it's because there's no place for them in this world that you've created."

He looked at me with endless eyes, then continued.

"I'd recommend a tsunami to set things straight. You gotta destroy to create. And from the looks of this place, it could use some good devastation. Now, you got any questions?"

I stared, speechless, a lost look in my eyes.

"The only difference between you and me, kid, is that I know I'm an illusion. Now quit your self-loathing and make your dreams come true. This world, it's all for you."

The raven flew off while I wondered which part of myself to take the wrecking ball to first.

The Fire Burns

A boy on the school bus puts his mouth to the window and huffs to fog up the glass. She imagines that he imagines himself as a dragon, blowing fire into the sea and creating worlds of fog and steam. The boy places his finger to the glass, pauses, pensive, draws a web, and then a spider. He then draws a line from the spider to the edge of the fog canvas. He needs more space to work with so he takes a deep breath in and lets out another dragon's breath. He continues the line from the spider to a crescent he paints with his artist's fingers. He finishes his artwork with stars around the crescent. It's the moon. And then he signs his work. Riley.

All this took the boy no more than a minute, but it would stay written and drawn on her mind until her final years, though, of course, she could not know it at this point. She was 29. Actually 29, not the perpetual 29 of most women in their 30s. Her name was Judith, but she never let anyone call her that. Jude, she would firmly, but courteously correct anyone who made the mistake.

Jude stands on the corner of 3rd and Alcott, waiting for the little man of light to open her path across the busy street. When she looks away from the boy, Riley, she sees that she has missed the walking man. The hand of no's and don'ts is already up and counting down 10, 9, 8... She scurries across the intersection at double time, awkwardly in her high heels. She hates high heels, but she didn't think flats would cut it today.

She is already five minutes late to the most important interview in her life to date. It would be the third most important interview in her life overall. Each time she had an interview from then on the memory of the boy and his ephemeral art would always be with her, though she would not grasp the full connections and the meaning until just moments before her last breath. But again, she could not see her future, she barely grasped her present, and she preferred to forget her past, at least at this point.

On the ten minute walk to the Confluence Building, where Bartleby and Associates had their corporate office she tries not to think of earlier this morning. She had woken next to Eric, as she had for the last year and a half, and she had looked at him. She looked at his stubble, thinking of the way it tickled her when he kissed her, hating how it felt on her neck when they embraced. She looked at his short, dirty blond, bed-messed head of hair. He had a great head of hair, she was sure he would hold on to it into his old age. And then she thought of his old age. She saw him coming home from work, his children jumping up to hug his neck, one showed him a spider he had caught that day, trapped in a jar. He smiled at them, proud, satisfied in his legacy. She saw him put down his briefcase. His wife waiting for him with a glass of bourbon that she handed to him along with a kiss. She saw the back of his wife's head, long blonde hair. Jude's hair was brown.

If she passed the interview and if she took the job she would be moving. She did not know where, she would have a number of choices. She had talked to Eric about it. He was prepared to uproot and transplant with her. He had a small website development business that he could take with him. He might lose a few clients, but he could gain more just as easily. He was prepared to make the sacrifice. Was she ready to accept it?

A block away from the Confluence Building, she passes by Carter Elementary. Without intending to, she scans the playground for Riley. The spider and the crescent moon still fresh in her mind. Was the spider sending a web to the moon so she could climb up? Was the spider trying to leave Earth? Or was the spider trying to pull the moon down to Earth? This would take much more strength, and there would be consequences, repercussions for shifting the heavenly bodies. She imagines that she can ask Riley all these questions and he will answer in some indefinite, innocent way that only a child can answer philosophical nothings.

To her surprise, she sees him, or she thinks it's him. She was paying much more attention to the drawing than the boy. She is about to call his name, not thinking of how strange or alarming it might be, when she sees him pull out a matchbook. He squats in a hidden corner of the playground, school hasn't started yet and the only person who can see him is Jude. She watches him gather a pile of dead leaves. She knows, as a responsible adult, she should say something, or let one of the teachers know. But instead, she pauses, pretending to check her cell phone and half hides behind a lamppost.

He looks around clandestinely, a guilty smile creeps across his lips. He lights one match, it sputters out. He lights a second, and it burns his finger, he curses. When he lights the third match, he places it gently on top of the pyre of leaves. He watches it catch fire and he seems to be holding his breath. Jude is holding her breath. Then the bell rings. He jumps up, puts the matchbook back in his pocket and runs to his classroom.

In his rush he does not put out the fire. Jude watches it for a moment longer, and then she walks away to her interview, knowing what must be done. She does not think in thoughts, she thinks in images as old as cave paintings, and she thinks in knowings, bone-deep and primal. She thanks the boy, Riley, not for the last time.

The fire burns, alone and unwatched.

Make Way for Ducklings

Up with the sun. A glass of warm lemon water and a brief stretch. Then Joanna is out the door. It's a crisp and bright spring morning when she steps outside, and there's a thickness, a dampness to the air that feels so out of place here. She presses play on her phone and lets the booty bass and synthesized sounds of her Spotify workout station drive her forward. It's not her typical choice of music, to say the least. Joanna says that it's motivation for her to get the jog over quicker, to run harder. That's what she tells her fiancé anyways, but some part of her likes the thump and thud of the unconscious beats, the hip swaying, illiteracy of the music. Though she would never say so out loud.

She jogs down the hill, careful steps over jagged, bent and battered city sidewalks. She does not look left or right as she passes the construction site. The workers just arriving, sleep still in their eyes, energy drinks in hand. But they are never too tired to stare after her and occasionally attempt a futile whistle or catcall. Joanna tells herself that one of these days she's going to really let them have it. She imagines herself turning around, calling one of these men out, saying the perfect words that will bring shame to him and the men who silently stand by. She envisions nearby neighbors hearing her words and cheering for her as she jogs away triumphantly. And none of these men will ever objectify or dehumanize another woman ever again.

Steady strides take her past a small park. Homeless men shaking out their blankets look after her too, but not in the same way as the construction workers. Every morning Joanna feels a soft stab in her chest as she sees them. Every day she feels her heart in a tug-o-war of guilt and gladness. She thinks about how she would help if she had the money that many of the people in this city have. She feels grateful for what little she does have, realizing how privileged she still is, feeling guilty for wanting more.

Joanna passes the thirty foot high milk jug and thinks about the lines that people form around the block, just to get a single scoop of this ice cream. She continues down the hill and crosses the highway. She always tries to breathe in as shallowly as possible. She jogs steadily on to the river. Her normal path is closed by construction, so she takes the bridge over the swollen river and meanders down a zigzagging trail that puts her on the other side of the construction.

The rain has been relentless the last several weeks. Unseasonal, atypical and unprecedented. The river broke its boundaries two weeks ago and it continues to press higher and higher up, erasing the banks that had held it in place for so long. Joanna passes a group of women jogging. She sees one who she knows and says hello. They exchange brief "how do you do's" and continue on their own trajectories. The woman Joanna knew in the group is a multi-millionaire. Joanna imagines the group of women are all rich as well, just meeting up for their multi-millionaires' jogging club. She looks down at her worn and weary jogging shoes. Joanna fights back pangs of jealousy and runs on.

This is her favorite part of the jog. The roaring river beside her, already overgrown with grass, weeds and brambles. On the other side is an amusement park, roller coasters rising in serpentine sprawls, like giant centipede skeletons. She jumps, for a moment breathless, as a man exiting the bushes startles her. He is unkempt and haggard. He drags his sleeping bag behind him and places it on his cart. Joanna jogs past, stepping off the path to avoid a section flooded by the river. At 2.5 miles, according to her phone's jogging app, she turns around and heads back the way she came.

Joanna wonders for a moment how far the women's multi-millionaires' club jogs. Not as far as her, she thinks to herself, they probably have shopping excursions and pedicure appointments to get to. Joanna stops at the flooded section of the path again. A mother duck and her ducklings are swimming up from the river to rest in the calm pool. The baby ducks are heart-wrenchingly cute and comical in their awkward movements. Joanna is so engrossed in the ducklings that she doesn't notice the homeless man standing beside her with his cart.

He is the same man she passed just before who startled her as he emerged from the bushes. He is wild and crazy-eyed, but Joanna does not feel unsafe. They both look at the ducklings, letting soft sighs escape from their mouths.

"You jusht don't shee many ducklinsh anymore, do ya?" says the man.

"No," Joanna responds, "you don't."

They watch the ducklings bob and waddle for a minute more before Joanna continues on.

"Thanks for that," she says to the man. "You have a nice day."

"You too, missh."

She waves goodbye to him and doesn't think about guilt or jealousy or gladness for the rest of her jog. She just thinks about little baby ducklings. If everyone could just stand around and stare at ducklings, it wouldn't matter who you were or what you'd done, or what you have or whether or not you deserved the hand you'd been dealt. All that would matter were the cute, fuzzy quacks of the ducklings.

Literary Refugee

Where do the words go when no one is in need of them?
When poets get pragmatic and put down the pen, to search
for steady girlfriends and submit their resumés. There has to
be some safe house, or an isolated island where words like
cadence and *grist*, and *pinhole* go when they're not being
chewed on by some starving artist.

No, I won't believe that words just wait patiently and
disappear into the meta-nothingness of Plato's whispy
world. There has to be somewhere for words like *lunar*, and
viaduct and *terse*. If they don't have a safe place they'll be
swallowed by the next Stephen King novel. If they are just
abandoned on the corner like some raving derelict they'll
end up pitied charity cases placed in the false shelter of
Madonna's next children's book.

I won't stand for it.

I won't let it happen.

So until the world renounces their bubblegum-content-
driven media, until the publishers banish their banal novels
and verbosely rancid memoirs. Until all nations unite to
clothe, feed and shelter every adjective that can replace
beautiful, every noun that can replace *love*, and every verb
that can stand in for *ache*. Until all words and phrases are set
free from the barbarisms of mediocrity and saved from a life
as literary refugees.

Until then I have no other option than to open the doors
of my heart and mind as a neutral halfway home, a relatively
safe haven. And I promise to do everything I can to offer
shelter and a place to sleep, a crust of bread and what wine I

can keep to the desolate words that want nothing more than to be spoken aloud or put in some tale.

I will give a home to every word I can, but these measly morsels of song and story, these crude pages and unpublished chapbooks will hardly suffice until the day we hear words like *remedy, ambrosia, hallelujah* and *sovereignty* ring out.

Shaq Attack

It was one of those warm summer nights when trouble came calling like a dark breeze from the land of mayhem and boredom and teenage disquiet. The real trouble was, this was every night for us. But on this night we had a plan, beyond just scrounging together our change to buy a couple dozen eggs.

We had Shaq.

The previous day I had entered Burger King under the guise of buying a whopper. I left the restaurant with a life-size cardboard cutout of Shaquille O'Neal. The manager chased me out, but Kevin was standing watch with the trunk of his car popped. We ran like bandits and laughed like lunatics as we drove back to our robber's den, Jeremy's house.

We drew all over Shaq, gave him a Hitler mustache, stabbed out his eyes with a butter knife, carved a pentagram into his forehead, you know, kid stuff. When night fell and the coyotes began to howl we left our hideout in Cobos's red Ford Taurus.

We first took Shaq to a friend's house, a girl we all had a mutual crush on. The air was electric with hazard and elation. The streetlamps burned their carbon glow on the suburban streets and we danced with our shadows through the summer night. We rang the doorbell and hid behind a parked car across the street.

Her mother came out, we stifled our mirth as she looked this way, then that and cursed our unknown names. Our friend came out next and laughed, her mother joined in. We revealed ourselves and reveled in a prank well pulled. We thought the night would continue like this.

A couple more doorsteps, but no one was home, or no one answered. That was when we decided to find a house we knew for sure was occupied. We arrived in an unknown cul-de-sac to a house full of people. We perched Shaq on the doorstep, all seven feet and satanic. We rang the doorbell and waited in snickering anticipation.

The door burst open. A volley of shouts erupted. A dozen or so young men got into suped-up Asian sports cars, revved the engines and pealed their tires, on the hunt for those responsible for the Shaq attack.

They shined their headlights on us like cold wolves' eyes and we ran like deer. We hopped fences, crashed into bird baths and skidded over trampolines. Every corner we turned we could hear the roar of engines and the high-pitched thunder of those idiotic mufflers.

After 20 minutes of running on foot, we made it back to Cobos's Taurus. We ducked, unseen, into the coupe and started the engine. We thought we had escaped, but then realized we had boxed ourselves in. The only way out was right past the house we had Shaq attacked. We inched forward, not wanting to alert anyone to our presence. Ten yards or so from the exit to the cul-de-sac, one of the rice burners pulled in. They saw us, we saw them.

"Fuckin' go, Cobos!"

Rubber burned asphalt and we ran like the devil was at our heels. Stop signs be damned. Cobos rode the dips like a roller coaster, even as he bottomed out and sparks flew. We were doing 60 or 70 in a residential neighborhood, and the sports car behind us was doing the same. They never trailed by more than a few yards, then we came to an intersection that would make or break this chase. It was a blind right turn on Smoky Hill Road, a busy main vein of Aurora. It was a three-way game of chicken: us, our enemy and the traffic ahead. Cobos called all of their bluffs.

101

"Oh shiiiiiittttt!!!"

We all screamed in unison. Cobos slowed down only enough to keep from rolling the car. Horns blared, tires squealed, we all collectively pissed ourselves. Cobos had managed to wedge himself like a slice of cheese right between a sandwich of two cars that would have killed us, or we would have killed them. I looked behind us at our pursuers. They had screeched to a halt at the intersection. We hooted and hollered as we drove off triumphant into the black night that was our shelter, our guardian.

We had narrowly escaped with our freedom, our lives. And we had learned no lessons.

Destiny's Pocket Watch

Julian opened the door of his Buick LeSabre and untied his shoe before walking into the Goodwill. In the ten yards or less that he had to walk to the door he feigned ignorance of his dangling laces. But with every step Julian had to fight a cringe, and a neurotic repulsion he had to the thought of something so close to him out of place, dysfunctional, disorderly. He opened the door for a woman and her screaming child, glanced at his watch, and he entered the store.

He pretended to browse the wares for a minute, looking through wicker baskets with a weaver's eye. He looked at his watch to make sure that precisely two minutes and twenty-two seconds had passed since he entered the store. Then he went to the front case, which held odds and ends like jewelry, shoes, purses and such that the thrift store thought too valuable to leave unsecured. In this case, underneath a pair of moth eaten opera gloves was a gold pocket watch. This pocket watch held the answers to a million riddles inside that Julian had to know.

It was only $99.99, but it was money that Julian did not have, and would not have in any foreseeable future, unless that pocket watch was in his possession. He bent down to tie his shoe. Reaching into his shoe Julian carefully removed a lock pick and a tension wrench. He made sure the sales clerk was busy at the cash register and otherwise occupied. Then he began to work. He had watched dozens of YouTube videos on the proper technique and he had done his research on the design and model of this particular lock. He was an out-of-work watchmaker and an antique clock repairman by trade, not a cat burglar, but his profession had taught him a steady hand and a deep affinity for working with the small, delicate inner world of mechanisms.

Julian had the lock open in 7 seconds. His tools were stored back in his shoe and his shoe was tied in 15 seconds. But the sales clerk was quick and adept at her work at the cash register.

"Did you need to see something in the display case?"

Julian had to focus and steady himself on the quivering hairs of her upper lip to keep from running, or going catatonic, or screaming out his guilt. If he looked at her broad, wide nostrils, he would be lost and the war-torn mud holes of her abysmal brown eyes would certainly swallow him whole and send him into a prison of desolation. It was the small micro-verse of the single mustache hair just above the mountainous mole on the left side of her lip that kept Julian's mind scalpel-sharp, laser-focused. He spoke to that mustache hair, and that mustache hair alone when he responded.

"What color tag was on sale today?"

"Green."

The word came out with the stench of stale cigarettes, a smell that had always been calming and reassuring to Julian. It reminded him of his mother.

"Ah, in that case... no."

He turned abruptly and perused the books, all the while keeping his eye on the register and the artificially peach-haired, broad bosomed woman behind it. He watched and waited, knowing that if anyone else came up to the display case and asked to see inside they would find the lock open and his guilt would be wide open with it. He imagined a SWAT team and a rabid canine unit descending upon him. He found a cobweb in the back corner of a bookshelf to look into and find his peace, his center. The cobweb had several gnats, a price tag, and a candy corn inside its wispy world. When he looked back at the register a new customer was just dropping her musty clothes and gaudy paintings of landscapes on the counter. Now was his only chance.

He returned to the display case. The sales clerk cast a wet, leering eye in Julian's direction, but not a suspicious glance, it was the look she would give to a beggar or a stray dog. Julian pretended to be tying his shoe again, he was not enough of a scam artist to think of anything else at that moment. He pushed the glass aside, the case squeaked and almost sent Julian careening backwards with its intensity, but neither clerk nor customer took notice. Julian's bony, nimble fingers reached in the display case and took hold of the end of the pocket watch's chain. He pulled slowly and the opera gloves danced in response. He pulled again and the watch clinked against the glass. Again, the noise was like a trash can marching band to Julian, but it met with a beep from the price gun on the register. It took Julian one more slow, steady pull on the chain to release the pocket watch from the display case. And then there was the frantic, infinite moment when it was in limbo, out of the display case, but not yet in his pocket. That moment, for Julian, was like a thousand days in Alcatraz, an eternity in the prison of a genie's lamp. When he finally had the watch in his pocket his heart was beating like a techno thunderstorm. He could hear nothing over his pulse, over the blood throbbing like an erupting volcano through his frail body.

He actually did fall backwards this time when light and sound caught back up to him.

"Hey! Hey! You there? I said 'did ya' change yer mind about the display case?' Jeeze, they don't pay me enough for this crap."

Julian picked himself up and managed to mumble a 'no thank you' or some other similar noise before he was retreating like a wounded giraffe out the door. He could feel the power of the thing in his pocket and the ticking of his destiny inching closer.

Occupied

He sits, he listens. Every step of the wind, every twitch of the house, he leaps up into himself, he retracts. Sweat glistens from his forehead like a tropical microclimate and runs down his face and torso like the Amazon. His perspiration makes the seat nearly frictionless and he has to dig his feet into the plush, carpeted rug beneath him just to stay on his throne.

He watches the door. He knows he locked it, or did he? And there is also a ring and a hook which he has secured. But what are locks to a thief or a voyeur? A scopophiliac, he had looked up the word because the fear of such a person had haunted his dreams and his private waking moments for so long. Someone who could at this very moment be watching from the crack in the door, or the window. Someone who could see into his most secret self, his most sacred ritual. His breath is shallow and ragged, every muscle in his body clenched. His poor sympathetic nervous system, a little too sympathetic. Every time he enters this particular room for this particular somatic obligation his body courses so quickly and so fully with stress hormones that the most harrowed junky on the streets could hardly be as toxic. His heart beats like a punk rock drum set, fast, furious and cacophonous, struggling to provide blood and oxygen to a body choking and strangling on fear and paranoia.

He tries breathing. It doesn't help. His diaphragm is somewhere up near his ears. He tries to visualize a safe place, a secret fortress, but all he sees are eyes watching him. He's had four cups of coffee and no breakfast, he's practically ready to explode, but his fear is stronger than his will, stronger than even the needs of his body. He waddles over to the door and makes sure it's locked for the third time. He peers up at the frosted glass window, searching for shadows. Nothing but the leaves of a tree dancing in the sunlight.

He returns to his seat, wipes it down before he gets on it again. He sits and revisits the steps Dr. Remiel taught him. Breathe, breathe, full breath in, full breath out. Keep breathing, visualize a mountain valley filled with wild flowers next to a crystalline stream. This was the vision Dr. Remiel had created for him after asking him of his fondest childhood memories. He sees this place now. He feels himself sitting in the soft grass, watching the stream dance past. Eyes closed, he listens to the water's music, feels the warmth of the sun, the kiss of the wind.

Then he hears a noise. He opens his eyes in the vision. A grizzly bear is towering over him, just on the other side of the stream. And then from deep within the bushes two evil eyes prey on him, a snake slithers toward him. And higher up on a hill a mountain lion prowls toward him. He hyperventilates, he nearly screams out loud. He wants to run, but he is trapped in the vision. The beasts creep toward him, step by step, as if enjoying the slow torture they inflict on him. They smile their horrid smiles, teeth and fangs dripping wet with the desire for his flesh. They are so close he can smell the carcass stench of their breath. They open their mouths, hot breath, ready to devour him.

Then a knock on the door. He leaps off the porcelain and bites his tongue until he tastes blood.

"O-o-occupied..." He stutters, the sweat trickles on his brow and the rest of his body.

The muscles in his body, tense before, are now contracted tighter than a boa constrictor over every bone and sphincter in his body. He is ready to give up, though the pain in his bowels is excruciating. He is just about to get up when a rumble sends a shockwave through his body. He sits straight up, as though his body is finally about to win the war with his mind. But then a cat walks by the window. Its shadow passing by like a visit from death itself. The shudder that had coursed through him downwards now reverses itself and retreats back up. He bends over, crippled, as a sword of fire stabs through his guts.

When he bends over, a piece of lint from his pants catches on to the tip of his nose. He is curled over for a long time, aching all over like he is stricken with an acute case of dengue fever. With his head down between his knees he sees more visions. He is in a hospital, doctors, nurses and interns gathered around poking and prodding him, taking notes, staring, staring, while he sits on the bed, a bedpan beneath him and the pain in his gut tearing him apart. He sees a snake, a long brown snake, taking its time slithering toward him while he lays paralyzed.

He sits up quickly, trying to shake off the visions, wiping his brow off with the back of his hand. He feels an itch on his nose. He goes cross-eyed looking at the piece of lint. He is about to brush it off when the prickle of a sneeze flutters through his nose. He lifts his head up, eyes watering.

"A-a-a-ACHOOOO!"

The sneeze erupts with a volcano's force. He looks down, overwhelmed with relief, but then a new and even greater horror grips him as he turns left, then right, then around frantically.

"NO, NO, NOOOOOOOOOOOOO!" He curses the Heavens.

No toilet paper.

Quitter

"That's it, Morty." Noah put his nail gun down forcefully. It fired off and somewhere in the distance of the skyscraper's skeleton a piercing scream echoed. Neither men seemed concerned.

"Whatter ya' doin' Noah?" Vincent Mortimer picked up the gun and handed it back to Noah. Another shot fired. Somewhere above them a chorus of muffled curses and a hissing of compressed water through pipes.

"Who do I talk to about quitting? I'm not doing this anymore."

"Aw hell, this again?" Morty's non-lazy eye scrutinized Noah like a cop while the other eye looked out at the grey skyline, following a pigeon.

"Yes, this again. It's not right. Don't you ever wake up and wonder why you're here?"

Noah was getting himself worked up again. Morty knew the signs, pacing, fingernail biting, hair pulling, and Noah always came within a few inches of the edge of the building, 30 floors up.

"Noah, you're gettin' mighty close to the edge. Why dontcha come on over here and sit down. I'll pour ya' a cuppa coffee and you can tell ol' Mort what's the real matter."

Noah paced on, not hearing Morty's suggestions.

"This morning I woke up from a dream about flying. We were workin' on this building. Like we've been doing for the last four years. When all of a sudden we hear a holler and everyone turns their heads just in time to see..."

He stopped talking for just a second and placed his hands between two steel beams, leaning out and looking over the edge of the building.

"Someone had jumped. We all run to see him fall to his death with a sort of sick interest. He's about to hit the ground and our eyes are all stuck like we couldn't pull them away even if we wanted to. Everyone is saying something under their breath, praying to God, or cursing Him. And just as we all cringe, expecting to hear that telling thud, we don't hear anything. Everyone looks down and there's no body, no blood. Someone yells 'There he is!' We look up and he's flying now. He's waving to us and he's soaring over the city. He tosses his helmet away behind him and then he's gone forever. Freer than any of us will ever be."

Noah sagged, slumped against a concrete column. Morty trotted over like a medic to hand him his thermos full of black coffee.

"Now Noah, it's just a dream. You shouldn't let yourself git so worked up over a dream."

"Just a dream? What's that even mean? This is just a building. And we're just doing a job. Sometimes I think dreams are the only thing that really matters. Sometimes I just—"

Both men heard the shouts. They turned their heads just in time to see something fall. It could have been anything. Noah and Morty glanced at each other and then stepped warily to the edge to look down.

Broken Wishbones

I was the boy who ran out of the house on Thanksgiving to knock on every neighbor's door.

"Can I have your wishbone?" I asked them one by one.

Every face looked back at me with a mixture of confusion, amusement and pity. I got the wishbones. I think because they knew I would not leave their doorstep until I had watched them at least try to appease me. I brought them all back home and began to construct a wishing artifact. It was all the wishbones I had found, 14, strung together with dental floss. My family looked at me the same way all the neighbors did, though there was a more furrowed knot of understanding in their eyebrows, and deeper creases of worry around their lips.

I wore the wishbone necklace for weeks after, until Carla Burgeon ripped it off my neck and stepped on it, crushing each and every wish. I can pinpoint that moment as the defining turn in my life. The bone-crunching fall of grace. The snapping of innocence, and hopes, and dreams. I have never forgiven her, even though her mother died in middle school in a car accident, even though she became fat and pimply and unpopular in high school. I truly believe that the wishbone necklace was like some sacred relic, some protective amulet. It held my hopes in frail bird bones. It encircled my self in a ring of power and possibility. I had no knowledge of magical rites or incantations when I made the necklace, but there is a stronger, deeper river of alchemy stemming from a child's purposeful, unconscious acts. Unknowingly I had fused my pure, child self into the wishbones and Carla had been the demon of ravaged virtue and desolation.

I did not know at the time that a part of my soul had been shattered. The changes that shed their way through me were subtle, embedding their poison in me gradually over the years. Two twisting snakes of shadow and fate coiled around me, slipped through me and possessed me. At the age of 12, I saw the first inevitable hiss of the darkness in me. I was walking home from school, it was a gray day bitten by the freeze and silence of winter. I first smelled it, it hit like a whip, warm and acrid and foul. I looked down, I could actually see steam coming off the pile of feces at my feet. I looked up to see the dog who had left that rotten pile of himself behind wagging away through the park. With no conscious thought or intention I found a shard of ice and I lifted the pile off the ground. The smell was ripe and sickening, but something in me was dancing and rejoicing in it. I walked with careful, winter-practiced steps to the door of a boy from school. This boy had never wronged me, he was actually a friend in the forgotten days of elementary school. But now he was teased and shunned and I had no pity in my heart for him.

I still remember opening his screen door with the stealth of a practiced assassin. I smeared dog poop on his door handle, on his door step, and what was left of the mess I placed in the mailbox. Afterwards, I walked away as nonchalant as I had been walking before, maybe even calmer and more confident. And I was whistling a tune.

There are some who say that life is a choice. Every day, every moment we decide who we are and whether we shall walk the path of darkness or light. I find no such free will. My course was laid out for me, my choices serve only to suffocate candles and darken light in every act. I do not know what I would have been had my wishbone necklace not suffered its wrathful fate. Or had I never been possessed by the innocent desire to knock on my neighbors' doors that

Thanksgiving, begging for their unused, disregarded wishes. I can only speculate that the shadow side of life had plans for me from the very beginning and I have no say in my own freedom.

As the years crept by I gave in to the snakes' venom. I could not find the strength to overcome their bidding and so I found myself taking pens from banks, not tipping for coffee, and lying about what I had done over the weekend. Small, harmless things, or so they may seem, but the devil is in the details. And the details of my life were amassing into an unholy scripture of black verses. When I left my gum behind in drinking fountains, or worse, when I spit from the tops of high places, imagining someone's head as the landing zone. When I passed gas in the elevator and let the poor child holding his mother's hand take the blame. And the countless times I pressed the handicap button to open doors for me.

It is no proud memoir I write of my life's accomplishments. I speak only to release the tar and poison, though only for a moment. Even now as I write I feel the cold, dead grip of sloth and fear clutching at me. This life's path is the blade of a knife. Stay on the narrow path, lest you find my fate.

Blue Forgotten

"So let me get this straight. You want me to shoot you. In the head. And then you think I should shoot myself right after?"

She just stared at the steel sky, looking as hard as metal herself. But Saul could see that she was trembling, ever so slightly.

"And you think that St. Peter at the Pearly Gates, or wherever it is you think you're going, will overlook your death as a suicide because of what? A clever scheme, a deal you made, some damn semantics?"

Brynn just stared harder at the coffin of clouds. Put more effort into stilling the tremors coursing through her body. It looked painful. Saul ached for her.

"And what do you think your judgment will be for what you made me do? Making the man who loves you pull the trigger for you because you're holding on to some Catholic superstition about suicide. Do you really think it matters at this point? Why worry about Hell, it can't be any worse than this!"

Saul looked around him at the empty cupboards, the blood stained counter tops. The dust, debris, mold, mildew, vomit and shit that caked the world like some twisted vegetation. Every step, every breath ended in so much annihilation it was like the earth had turned over its green and gold blooming things for a nature that stemmed from death, from the bowels of despair. It no longer made him want to be sick, he accepted it the way an inmate eventually accepts life behind bars.

"And you think killing myself will just be that easy? You think I haven't thought about it a million times? I would've done it months ago, but it's just not something I'm going to do. No religion, no bullshit fear of punishment, it's just not something I will allow. I'm in this life until the end. I have no special love or hope that keeps me, but I will not take my own life. I don't have any explanation or reasoning, hell, I don't understand it myself. It's just something I've always known."

He looked at Brynn now and she was weeping and crumpled. The trembling had stopped, her face was a wet, grimy smudge. She still looked beautiful, he thought to himself.

"So the answer is no. I won't do it," he finished.

Brynn kept staring at the gray sky. It had been gray for ages, ever since the Last Day. Day and night were now just different shades of gray.

"I remember the blue," Brynn whispered.

"What?" Saul asked, confused and worried that she was really losing it. "What blue?"

"The sky." Her voice was like a whisper from a graveyard.

"Tell me about it." Saul just wanted to keep her talking.

"It was so soft, so light. It seems like a dream now. It's fading away, more and more every day. It's hard to remember it, but I've been holding on to it. I don't know if I can see it right in my head anymore. It was a really light blue, right? It was like clouds got mixed with the ocean and the color that came out was this washed out, creamy blue that brightened your eyes and lit up the whole world. Do you remember?"

"I do," said Saul, "sometimes I think I'd rather forget. It would make life easier now if we could just forget, just pretend like this is the only way the world could be, the only way it ever was."

"I've tried to forget, Saul." Brynn kept talking in that same lost voice. "I've tried so hard, but it won't go. It's starting to fade, though. Maybe once that blue is completely gone from me, I'll be better. What do you think?"

"Do you know why the sky was blue?"

Brynn didn't answer. Saul went on.

"It was because of how light reflected or refracted through the atmosphere. I was never the best at science, but I remember asking my mom and dad over and over again until they finally pulled out a textbook and answered me. I couldn't have been more than 5 or 6, but I still remember. Kind of. So the sun's light comes out in every color of the rainbow. But when it comes through the earth's atmosphere the light gets reflected, or scattered, or bounced around by the gasses and other stuff in the air. For some reason, I think it was because blue light has shorter waves or something, the blue light it was makes it through, and so we have a blue sky."

"Had." Brynn corrected.

"Yea, used to, I guess. But the laws of science haven't changed. Even though life has. There's gotta still be a blue sky out there somewhere."

"I don't want to believe in it anymore."

"Huh?" Saul asked.

"The blue. I don't want to think of it. I don't want to believe in it, or hope for it. I think it will be easier just not to."

"Will it help you to keep on? To keep moving with me, even though there might be nothing to move toward?" Saul asked.

"It might," Brynn answered, "help me up."

Saul took her hand and helped her stand. She took her pack and let it bite into her shoulders again.

"Let's go," she said.

Saul tucked the gun into his belt.

116

"Don't do that again. I don't know if I'll be strong enough to say no next time."

Brynn couldn't look at him, just stared ahead. She reached out for Saul's hand. They walked through the streets and sky of ash together, with no hope but each other.

Unpublished

Duct tape, one 15 foot rubber hose, Yamazaki whiskey, and a steak burrito from Chipotle, extra hot sauce. He wasn't doing this on an empty stomach. It wasn't a long list for such a permanent solution. He thought of adding more to the list, but couldn't find the justification. The more he thought about a short list, the more fitting it seemed. A short list, a short life, for the short end of the stick that he was given. But no melodrama, not tonight. He had promised himself that. He had spent his whole life crying out and beating his chest against the unfairness, the injustice. And for the first and last time, since he was taking the coward's way out, at least he would do it with a little dignity.

He opened the bottle first. Poured four fingers, and tossed in a cube of ice. He thought of picking out another, more traditional whiskey, but Yamazaki held in it the deepest flavor of nostalgia to him, the richest lingering of regret. The burn was smooth and clean and painless. He didn't want a harsh drink, just something easy and intoxicating to help it all go down.

Next he started in on the burrito. He had thought of other things to dine on for his last meal. As much as he enjoyed so many other dishes, this is what seemed most appropriate for the occasion. It was what he had probably eaten more often than anything in his life, what he craved when he was famished, what his dreams rested on when he was far away in lands that offered no serviceable burritos. It was so simple, so satisfying, so complete a package wrapped in a soft, warm tortilla. He was surprised by his hunger this night. He was expecting not to have much of an appetite, but he devoured the whole burrito before he even realized it was gone.

Well, down to business. He stepped heavily out to his car with the hose and the duct tape. He didn't really know how this was supposed to work. He assumed just the duct tape and the hose would be enough to get the job done. He assumed many things. He put the hose into the exhaust pipe. It was a little thin, he hoped that wouldn't be a problem. If he used enough duct tape to seal the hose to the exhaust pipe, with no places for the fumes to leak out, it should work. He used a quarter of the roll.

Next he ran the hose to the driver's side window. It was long enough, with just a little room to spare. When the cashier at the hardware store had asked him what kind of project he was working on, he just answered, "Fixing something that's been broken for a long time."

He went back inside to pour another glass of whiskey, six fingers this time. He wanted to make sure everything was in its place. The note was left sealed on the counter, inside was a will, of sorts. He had very little to leave behind, but he wanted to make sure certain sentimental items went to his family, and his few friends. The note was not long. He had spent so much of his life writing, he felt futile writing a drawn out suicide note. But he did make sure to leave a thorough, unmistakable grievance with his former publisher, letting them know that this was mostly their doing.

He returned to the car, slumped into the driver's seat and placed his glass of whiskey and the bottle on the dashboard. He pressed play on a mix that he had made earlier in the week. On another occasion it would have been a truly sublime creation, a compilation of his favorite songs from the last 32 years. Anyone in his generation would have listened to the mix and wept, laughed, raged, and sung along with their hearts spilling out. But this night it was a funeral dirge.

He turned the key in the ignition.

He took a deep draught of whiskey and let the loss of words drown him. His stories, the words yet unwritten, the words already on paper, but without an eye to read them, stillborn. He had so many sagas to share, so many wondrous worlds, but no one would ever know. He had never found a home for his words, had never found an audience. And at 32, he had decided that it had been long enough. If he hadn't found a way to share his works then they were either not good enough, or the world was not fair enough to allow him his voice. He had set a deadline, and this was it.

He had been picked up by a publisher, no one quite as grandiose as he had dreamed, but big enough, a stepping stone. When they pulled out on him at the last minute, well that was when he knew. There was no place for him or his writing in this world. Maybe the next.

Just then his phone buzzed. He forgot that he had kept it in his pocket. He was getting so tired now, so removed. He picked it up and answered without looking at the number.

"Hello," he slurred.

"Mr. Nielson? This is Drake, with Broken Jar Publishing. How are ya?"

"Suurrree," he mumbled.

"Listen, you sound busy, but I just wanted to tell you, we got things cleared up with accounting and we found a place for your book in next year's catalogue."

"Whaaaaa?"

"Mr. Nielson? I'm sure you're very busy. I have to go. More calls to make. But we'll be in touch. Congratulations again, Mr. Nielson. Sorry about the confusion. Well, you take care."

He dropped the phone. He reached for the door handle, but he was so weak, so tired. He couldn't gather enough strength to open the door. He fell asleep then, and put the period on his last sentence.

A Man Becomes a Tree

He was born a boy and he died a tree. And then he was born a tree, and it is suspected that he will die a tree. It was the day of his death/birth. He was in the bed of his brother's truck. He was staring at the sky and he was ready to rest. He could have never felt this content or at peace as a man.

He went to the Amazon as a college student for a summer course on anthropology. He was never going to become a professor. He was a poor student and his heart just wasn't in it. What his heart was in were people. He should have been a counselor, or an activist, or in human resources, it would have saved him from becoming a tree in the end. But what can one do? None of us knows what we want to be when we finally grow up.

So there he was, in the sticky, vivid heart of the Amazon eating, drinking, dancing and becoming close with the Marubo tribe. He became a little too close with one young maiden of the tribe, Yaminah. He never did discover her age. She could have been 18 as easily as 38. They had retired to the dense jungle for some privacy. Their kisses were just becoming urgent and frantic and frenzied when he felt a sharp pain in his foot. He looked down and saw a spike extruding from the hundred foot, thousand year old tree they had pressed against.

The natives called it the Jaguar Shaman Tree. They wouldn't go near it. Yaminah knew this, of course, but her squirming heart had obscured her vision, judgment and orientation.

In the backyard of his parent's home, the home he grew up in from just the seed of a human, he was planting his roots for his final resting place. The doctors told him that he had days, or weeks at most before he became totally immobile, petrified and completely—a tree. He decided, after narrowing his top options down to Giant Sequoia National Forest in Northern California, one particular lavender field in France that he had visited when he was 20, and the rain forest where he had first been infected, that his childhood home was the only obvious place.

His family and friends were gathered around. They carried his body as gently as they could on their shoulders to a freshly dug hole. The dirt looked warm, soft and comforting to him. When they placed him down, he let out the last sound he would ever make. It was a low, resonant, resounding sigh that reverberated from head to toe through those in attendance. When the last shovel full had been placed over his feet/roots, his eyes, now two knots, closed, and his face widened into a smile. Hard, rough bark was already forming around it.

What Jesus, Dinosaurs and Aromatherapy all Have in Common

I hear it in your voice, the way your larynx creaks like floorboards. I wonder if you hear my reply, "What now?" the same way I do, like the angry hornet's nest in our attic. We can never seem to keep the bastards from coming back, tried everything.

"It's a ticket," you say.

"Course it is." So predictable.

The city and county giveth and they taketh away.

"It says they can boot me."

"Well, I guess you gotta call, or pay."

You're sitting on the toilet while I float in the bathtub. I submerge, wishing it were deep enough to give me the bends when I come back up. At least something real enough to be a true threat.

"Is this all we've got?"

I say to no one.

"I'll call them tomorrow, I guess."

You close the seat and don't flush.

"Is this all there is?"

I say to no one again. I'm not the first to ask it and I won't be the last, but God damn, if this isn't the inanest, most melodramatic existence we've invented. Keeping survival at bay to be nagged to death by mediocrity.

Ah, just give it a rest, I say to myself as I dream of drowning in the tepid water, which was heated by dinosaur bones, infused with dead sea salt and the essential oils of rare and therapeutic plants.

Jesus may have walked on this water (or was it the Sea of Galilee? Same difference) now we import it to our bathtubs and float.

Prometheus

"Check it out," Leo beckoned Robbie over with a whisper and a clandestine gleam in his eyes.

He reached into his pocket and brandished the shiny, red Bic. It had its own inward glow, drawing the boys closer.

"I stole it from my dad," Leo bragged.

"What if he finds out?" Robbie had seen what Leo's dad could do when he caught Leo stealing, or lying, or talking too loudly, or doing anything that bothered him, really.

"He won't. He says every day that he can never find a lighter when he needs one. He's always losing them. He'll just think he lost this one too."

Leo stuffed the lighter back into his jeans, scrambling frantically in a futile attempt to look both casual and innocent. Robbie felt a boney hand on his shoulder.

"Hi, boys. Is anyone picking you up from school today?"

It was Ms. Brasch, spittle-flecked speech and old-person-breathed.

"Yes, Ms. Brasch," Leo responded, "my big brother'll be right outside. And he's going to walk both of us home."

Robbie looked to Leo. Leo looked to Robbie. Both nodded emphatically. She held both of their gazes for several breathless seconds.

"Very well, then. Off you go. Don't keep your brother waiting."

She walked off to scold more students. Robbie and Leo bolted as soon as her back was turned.

They walked out the front doors, then circled around to the back of the school. Through the playground, across the field, behind the dugout to the secret creek entrance. They looked around to make sure no one was watching them and then they ducked into the bushes.

Deep in the thick of their green, weedy, thistled fortress, Leo pulled out the lighter. Robbie used a stick to dig up their buried *Playboy*. Another stolen treasure from Leo's dad. He pulled the magazine from its plastic cover perused, and sighed. There was enough boy in him to mostly be confused, but enough growing adolescence to be thoroughly enraptured in wonder and mysterious arousal. Robbie was broken from his musing when Leo lit a corner of the *Playboy*.

"Hey, stop!" Robbie shouted, "What the hell!?"

Leo laughed, a little too enthusiastically.

"Relax, dude. I wasn't going to burn it, just wanted to get the corners a little bit."

Robbie looked at Leo like he was staring down a coiled viper.

"Let's go. I wanna show you something."

Leo was already exiting their hideout before Robbie had time to argue. He hastily buried the porno, then chased after Leo through a maze of cattails. When he found Leo, the boy was digging through an overgrowth of thick weeds.

"Leo, we shouldn't be here. This is the big kids hangout."

Robbie looked around nervously, ready to bolt at any minute.

"Relax, they're not off school yet." He dug deeper in the weeds, "And anyways, I'm looking for something," he huffed, "that I thought I—"

Leo emerged from the weeds triumphantly.

"There it is!"

He held a blue bottle of hair spray in his hands. He had the look of a kid in a candy store, or a kid with a bomb in his hands. For Leo, the looks were one and the same.

"Check this out!"

Leo held up the lighter, lit the flame and sprayed the hairspray. It leapt out like a billowing dragon's breath. Robbie jumped back. He was amazed and terrified. Leo laughed maniacally again.

"Leo, we shouldn't be doing this. We're gonna get in trouble."

Robbie backed away, almost hoping that the middle schoolers would come and find them. At least it might stop Leo. Leo pointed the hairspray toward Robbie and ignited it.

"Hey!" Robbie screamed.

"Relax, it's not gonna hurt you. Watch this."

Leo sprayed his hand with hairspray, then lit the flame. It burned and raced up his arm. He patted his arm down in the dry grass to put it out.

"Whoa! That was awesome!" Leo shouted.

He sprayed his arm again, with much more hairspray this time. He lit it and watched the flames dance up his arm.

"This must be how they do it in the movies!"

He danced around, trying to wave the fire out. He only managed to fan the flames. Then a look of true fear entered his eyes. He rolled on the ground, beat his arm on the grass. Eventually he put the flame out, but his skin was red and he was clutching his arm in pain. Tears welled up.

Robbie stepped toward Leo, but as he moved closer he saw the grass in front of him ignite. It was slow at first, he thought he could put it out by stomping on it. But more smoke poured out from hidden depths in the brown grass. Then flames licked at Robbie's pant legs. He jumped back.

"Run!" Robbie yelled to Leo.

Leo backed away, stumbling to his feet. Robbie and Leo looked back at each other one last time before running off in opposite directions.

Robbie ran until the stitch in his side brought him to the ground. He didn't know why, but he climbed a tall tree when he finally caught his breath. From high up he could see the smoke and dancing flames in the distance. He watched as neighbors came running out, shouting into phones. He stayed until the fire department arrived. They couldn't get their truck close enough. The best they could do was contain the spreading fire.

Guilt, dread, shame and other emotions that have no place in a child's heart began to seep into Robbie. He wanted to go home, hide under his covers, but he couldn't face his parents. He wanted to tell the firemen the truth, let them take him away, but he was not brave enough. He stayed in the tree until dusk came with its gossamer fingers of fading sunlight reaching into him. *I'm not coming down*, he said to himself over and over. *I'm never coming down*.

Acknowledgments

The following titles first appeared in the following journals:

A Sunrise to See Before You Die, *Twisted Vine Literary Arts Journal of WNMU*

Three Scenes, *River Poets Journal*

New York, New York, *The Harpoon Review*

Five Points, *ZO Magazine*

The Ganga, *Story Mondo as Laxman Jhula*

Same, Same, but Different, *Severine Literary and Arts Journal*

First Hitch, *Eunoia Review*

The Creek, *Eunoia Review*

Buick LeSabre, *Flash Fiction Magazine*

Foregone Conclusion, *Five 2 One Magazine*

Life Lessons of the Periodic Table, *Foliate Oak Literary Magazine*

Boys Will Be, *LitroNY*

Writers Make Terrible Partners, *Connotation Press* and reprinted in *Easy Street Magazine*

Nursing, *Crack the Spine Literary Magazine*

Rain Check, *101 Words*

Coyote's Last Days, *Connotation Press*

Corpus Corvidae, *Zero Flash*

Trophy, *Birdy Magazine*

Shaq Attack, *Connotation Press*

Quitter, *Spelk Fiction*

Broken Wishbones, *The Airgonaut*

Unpublished, *Birdy Magazine*

A Man Becomes a Tree, *Scrutiny Journal*

Bear Creek, *Pure Slush*

Thanks

To begin, I have to thank my parents for instilling in me a love of stories from an early age. Thank you Hannah, my wife, for supporting, encouraging, and giving me the kick in the pants I need on occasion. In no particular order, all of the following people helped make this book possible in large and small ways and all of you are deeply appreciated: Jack C. Buck, Kathy Fish, Robert Vaughan, Nancy Stohlman, Paul Beckman, Sally Reno, Doug Matthewson, Len Kuntz, Matt Potter, Patrick Cross, Max Winne, Daniel Grant, Tyler Morse, Tovio Roberts, Bud Smith, Ilana Masad, Steve Karas, Gay Degani, all the literary journals that somehow found my work palatable, all my friends and family, and most of all, you, dear reader. If I have forgotten anyone may my bones never rest in the ground.

About the Author

Levi Andrew Noe was born and raised in Denver, Colorado. He is a writer, a yogi, an entrepreneur, an educator and an amateur oneironaut. Levi has many passions, though writing will always be his one true love. He has traveled extensively through North America and Asia, and has an insatiable wanderlust. He practices and teaches yoga, and is the founder of Tall Tales Yoga, a story-based children's yoga program. He is the editor in chief and founder of the podcast *Rocky Mountain Revival, Audio Art Journal*. Levi won first prize in 2011 and 2013 in *Spirit First's* international poetry competition. His works have appeared in *Connotation Press*, *Ink, Sweat & Tears*, *The Harpoon Review*, *Litro Magazine*, *Pure Slush*, *101 Words*, *Twisted Vine Literary Arts Journal*, and *Japan Travel*, among others.

For more about the author visit http://leviandrewnoe.com

You can also say hi to him on Facebook and Twitter @LeviAndrewNoe

Other books from
Truth Serum Press

Luck and Other Truths
ISBN: 978-1-925101-77-5

What Came Before
ISBN: 978-1-925536-05-8

happyme@t.us
ISBN: 978-1-925536-07-2

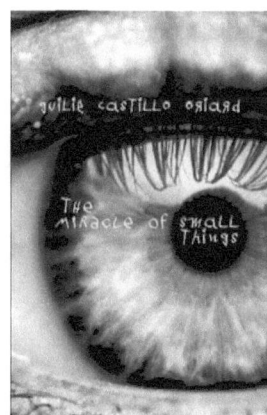

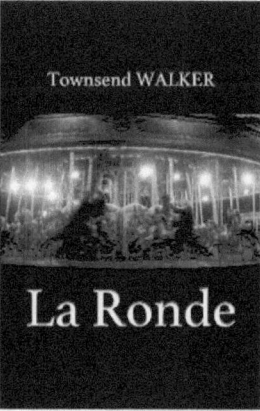

Miracle of Small Things
ISBN: 978-1-925101-73-7

La Ronde
ISBN: 978-1-925101-64-5

Based on True Stories
ISBN: 978-1-925101-75-1

Find all Truth Serum Press paperbacks and eBooks at
https://truthserumpress.net/catalogue/

www.ingramcontent.com/pod-product-compliance
Lightning Source LLC
Chambersburg PA
CBHW050826180626
46814CB00004B/1479